FINDING REDEMPTION

CHRISTINE GAEL

ANNA

THE DAY HAD STARTED SO well, Anna reflected as she poured herself a glass of scotch. A pedicure and a facial, topped off with a glass of bubbly and some sibling time to send her newly discovered half sister, Nikki, back off to Cherry Blossom Point in style.

And then Nikki's nineteen-year-old daughter, Beth, had shown up out of the blue, and things had gotten a whole lot more complicated. As far as Nikki knew, Beth had no idea about Anna's existence. Her showing up in the middle of their spa day and announcing she was there to see her new aunt had thrown a major wrench in the works.

Anna shot a furtive glance toward her dining room table. Nikki and Beth sat across from one another, and, judging by their body language, things weren't going well.

What she wouldn't give for just a month straight of zero drama. No crazy highs, but also no soul-sucking lows.

Just some peace and quiet.

She turned back to face the side table that acted as a

mini-bar, and her gaze connected with the framed photograph above it. It was one of her favorites, a group of wolf pups on their first day out of the den. She had stayed in a tent on site for almost a week to get that shot, and had braved a pretty scary confrontation with Mama wolf in the process.

A bubble of laughter threatened her lips. She'd never exactly prioritized peace and quiet in the past and had the pictures to prove it.

Then again, that *was* part of it, wasn't it? All those times she had camped out in the wilderness with only wildlife for company. It wasn't just the bustle of travel and adventure she had been seeking all those years. It was a certain kind of peace, too. She'd loved the excitement of going to places she'd never been, making new friends, trying new foods and embracing new cultures, too. But it was those quiet moments that kept her going. The stillness of the woods, the bone-deep satisfaction of getting that perfect shot. She'd come home to settle in Bluebird Bay over a year ago to get some more of that. So far, though, it had been a total rollercoaster.

Her oldest sister Cee-cee had reinvented herself and created an amazing business following her divorce. Middle sister Stephanie had finally laid her late husband to rest after tracking down his killer — and had nearly gotten herself killed in the process. And as for Anna?

Anna had kicked cancer's ass.

They'd also lost Pop, which was still was a deep wound in Anna's heart. But for all the bad, there had been a lot of good, too. Each of them had found love. Even Anna, who had thought that she would never settle down with a man, much less a grandfather — albeit a young, handsome grandfather —

like Beckett. They shared a house together, and she'd become a de facto grandma to toddler, Teddy.

Then, just when Anna's life felt full to bursting, Nikki had blown into town and announced that she was Anna's sister and that Anna had a whole other family in Cherry Blossom Point. All her life, her biological father had lived just two hours away. She had siblings she'd never met. A brother and two sisters who were either apathetic or outraged at her very existence...

And one who wanted to meet her.

Anna turned to the table and blew out a sigh as she looked at Nikki.

The ebb and the flow of life. It took and it gave. She hoped Beth would be another gift.

Right now, though? She was looking pretty pissed off.

And rightly so.

Anna shook her head ruefully as she poured a second glass of scotch for Nikki and headed toward the table.

She set one of the glasses down in front of her sister and then turned toward her niece.

"How about a scotch, Beth?" Anna asked.

"Anna!" Nikki exclaimed. She seemed to be trying for righteous indignation, but a glimmer of humor sparked in her eyes, breaking through the abject misery for just an instant. "She's only nineteen!"

"Oh. Right." Anna cleared her throat. She wasn't about to tell her new niece that she'd had her first scotch way younger than that, or that she'd stolen it from Pop's bottle of Johnny Walker and replaced it with water. "Apple juice, then?" she asked brightly.

"Ew. I'm nineteen, not four," Beth muttered, folding her

3

arms over her chest so tightly, it was like she was afraid Anna was about to try to harvest her organs and sell them on the black market. "I'm fine...but thank you," she added in a gentler tone.

Interesting.

Despite being furious and hurt, it was against her nature to be outright rude. Keeping Beth in the dark about some stuff aside, Nikki had clearly done something right.

"So are you ready to talk now, or...?" Nikki trailed off, her face soft with concern as she studied her daughter.

After barging into the spa and demanding to know which of the Sullivan sisters was her Aunt Anna, Beth had been teary-eyed and silent, refusing to answer any of Nikki's questions to this point. Once they'd washed their faces and gotten dressed, Anna had brought them to her house in hopes that the privacy and the intimate setting would help her open up. She'd tried to leave the two of them alone to talk, but Beth had insisted she stay.

Anna took a seat beside Nikki as Beth leaned forward to lay her hands on the table.

"I've been ready to talk since I climbed into the cab on the way to the airport. I had this whole speech planned out and everything," Beth said, a hitch in her voice. "And then when I saw you...and her," she paused, jerking her chin toward Anna, "all I could think of was how you've lied to me for the past two months. You found out about Anna and you moved to Bluebird Bay without even telling me."

"I didn't move here!" Nikki exclaimed, shaking her head. "You knew I was coming here to visit. We still have our home in Cherry Blossom Point. You and I had a plan, remember? We were going to meet back home for

Thanksgiving break in a few days. Are you cutting class right now?"

Anna winced and took a sip from her glass. Probably not the best time to bring that up, given—

"You've got to be kidding right now!" Beth shot back. "Grandpa had an affair on Grammy, you have a secret sister, and, oh yeah, my father was stalking you and then killed himself, and you're asking me about my *classes*?" she demanded, her hazel eyes practically bugging out of her head. "You've been here forever, Mom. You told me that you wanted to kick back, relax, and spend some time at the beach, do some leaf-peeping, and get some space from Uncle Jack. A vacation is a couple weeks. It's been, like, two months or something. I got worried something was going on, so I—" Beth hesitated. "I called Aunt Lena to ask what you were really doing here."

Lena.

Anna felt a small surge of panic. She didn't want to think about her, or the other siblings she hadn't met. She had barely let Nikki in. She was glad that she had given the younger woman a chance, but the thought of them, a father still living...

Anna took another sip of her drink.

"You know what a terrible liar she is," Beth was saying. "Both times I asked, she got all flustered and basically hung up on me. That's when I knew for sure something was up. So I googled the town to see what I could find. It was in the Gazette. *Suicide in Bluebird Bay.* The ex-husband of Nikki Merrill, long lost sister to the Sullivan clan. The freaking newspapers knew before I did!"

"That must have been very painful to read, but I was

5

going to tell you everything," Nikki replied to her daughter carefully. "As soon as we saw each other in person, I was going to tell you..."

Nikki raised her glass to her lips with a shaky hand and sipped. Then, she took a deep, steadying breath before meeting her daughter's eyes.

"I'm just sorry you had to find out that way. Honestly, I needed to pull myself together first. I... it was rough. It was scary, and it took me a couple weeks to get my head on straight again."

"You could have died." Tears threatened to spill from Beth's eyes and she brushed them away with an angry fist. "You could have died, and I wouldn't have even known why you were here."

Nikki stood and rounded the table to close the distance between them, pulling Beth into a hug. The tension seemed to drain away as Beth collapsed against her mother and began to cry.

"It's okay to be sad," Nikki murmured. "It's okay to cry for him."

"I don't care about *him*! I care about you," Beth flared, sitting up straight in her chair. "He was never even there," she added more quietly.

"And now he never will be," Nikki said. "It's okay to grieve that, even if he wasn't a true parent to you. He never had the chance to get to know you. He missed out on a lot."

"He didn't *want* to get to know me," Beth said bitterly.

"To be fair, after we left, he didn't have the option. I had to keep us safe, even if that meant depriving you of-"

Beth cut her off. "You didn't deprive me of anything. You saved us both from a lifetime of abuse. I'm not sad about that. I'm upset that you didn't tell me about it all. But I'm here now, and...I want to spend my Thanksgiving break in Bluebird Bay," she told her mother, darting a glance at Anna.

"Why?" Nikki asked, staring down at her daughter in confusion. "Your friends are going to be back home, we have the house. I'm already packed. I was going to head there tomorrow to clean and put fresh sheets on the bed. We'll have Thanksgiving dinner at Aunt Gayle's, with cranberry sauce, and then we'll play Uno and eat pie until our pants bust. Nothing has to change, Beth."

"Everything *has* changed, Mom! I want to know what brought you here." She shot a look at Anna and then looked away. "I want to get to know my new aunt."

Anna felt an unexpected surge of warmth for the stubborn girl across the table. She flashed Beth a smile. "I don't blame you. I'm the cool aunt. Just ask my other nieces and nephews."

Nikki smiled in spite of herself, but her forehead creased with worry as she turned back to her daughter.

"Honey, we don't even have a place to stay. My... the place where I was living—" She broke off and tried again. "We can't stay there after what happened with your father. I've been staying with a friend, and—"

"A male friend?" Beth interrupted, narrowing her eyes.

Nikki slid heavily into the chair next to Beth's and blew out a long sigh.

Anna so did not envy her right now. Apparently, hell hath'ed no fury like a teenage girl who had been kept in the dark.

"Yes, a male friend. His name is Mateo."

7

"Mateo Velasquez?" Beth demanded. "The guy the article said was there when Dad shot himself?"

"That's him," Nikki said, her voice barely audible.

"He was your mom's landlord, sort of, and he lived a few houses down. He heard the commotion and came running to help," Anna interjected. Nikki gave her a grateful look, but Beth wasn't so easily dissuaded.

"And you're shacking up with him now?" she asked with the searing disdain that only a teenage girl could muster. "He's your boyfriend, right?"

Nikki's face was a mask of guilt.

"Great," Beth muttered. "More secrets."

"No secrets," Nikki protested. "I was going to-"

"Tell me in person on Thanksgiving. So you mentioned. You know that you're allowed to visit me when I'm in school, right? I'm not, like, locked in a cell with set visitation days."

Nikki stared at Beth like she had just been slapped, and the room went silent.

"Is...um, is anyone hungry? I could fix us some chips and gauc..." Anna trailed off, mentally kicking herself. Chips and guac was football Sundays pickings, not "*I just found out my father is dead and my mom has a boyfriend*" fare.

Maybe she should've went with tuna salad, or soup. Soup had a lot more gravitas as far as foods went...

"I'm not hungry," Beth said, swiping at the remnants of tears as she pushed herself to her feet. "Aunt Anna, can I use your restroom? I need to wash my face and stuff."

"Of course," Anna told her. "Just around the corner there."

Beth disappeared, and Nikki put her head down on the

table with an exaggerated thump and then banged it one more time for good measure.

"I was a firecracker at that age, too," Anna said gently. "Hell, I was a firecracker just a couple months ago when you got here. So angry that my parents had lied to me. So righteous in that anger. Give her a little time. She's strong. She'll figure it out."

"I get why she's mad. It was dumb, keeping it from her. I almost told her before I came here, but I let my brother and sister get in my head. They insisted there was no reason to drag these bones out of the closet. Jack was so sure you would send me packing, and we could kick this skeleton back into the dark and forget all about it."

"I guess Jack was wrong." Anna was beginning to suspect old Jackie-boy was wrong about a lot of things. "Because, here we are." She lifted her drink to Nikki.

Nikki managed another glimmer of a smile and held up her drink to clink with Anna's. "Here we are."

They both took a sip and Anna studied Nikki's face for a long moment.

"You know, you guys can stay here if you want. We have plenty of room. Beckett will be home in like an hour, and I can double-check with him if it makes you feel better, but I know he won't mind."

And neither would I, Anna added silently.

Her feelings towards Nikki had changed so quickly. She was surprised to find that she was open to getting to know this fiery new niece now, as well.

She liked her spirit.

"Thanks for the offer," Nikki said with a grateful smile. "But I think I'll find an Airbnb or something, give us some space to process...all of this. I have no idea how she's going to feel tomorrow, and I'm thinking we need some time alone to work through it. I truly appreciate it, though."

"If you change your mind, you know where to find me."

As Beth came out of the bathroom and Anna met her now-shuttered gaze, she couldn't help but wonder if this was going to be a little trickier than her new sister had hoped...

TODD

TODD TOOK his time on the drive through town, enjoying the view. The trees were mostly bare, but a few stubborn branches clung to the last of their color. Fake foliage was out in abundance; shops and houses were decked out in Thanksgiving decorations—mostly oversized paper leaves that celebrated the all-too-short leaf-peeping season in Maine. In the distance, gentle waves lapped at the shore.

The familiar scenery, combined with the relaxing music he'd cued up on the radio in his Jeep, made for a welcome respite from the daily bustle of the clinic. He loved being a veterinarian and couldn't even remember a time when he wasn't tending to injured animals. Even as a small child, he'd always been the one to bring home the squirrel that fell from its nest or the cardinal with an injured wing. Taking over his mother's clinic was a lifelong dream come true. What he hadn't counted on was the stress. Even his dreams lately were full of botched surgeries and dizzying lines of code from the software he'd written for the clinic.

He couldn't deny it. The pressure was intense.

It wasn't just his patients and their families counting on him, either. A couple of years after his father had died, his grandfather had told Todd to take his place at the head of the table. He'd been insulted on his mother's behalf, insisting that she was the head of their family, now. But underneath that anger, he had been nervous, too. Part of him felt like Pop was right in a much bigger sense than just sitting at the head of the table on Thanksgiving dinner.

His mother had been inconsolable after his father had passed, slowly coming apart at the seams. Her near-death encounter with his murderer a couple years later had pushed her almost past the point of endurance, and she'd turned to pills to cope. She'd been in recovery and was doing so well, teaching yoga classes, attending her meetings to ensure she didn't relapse. His little brother had come home, even if it wasn't under the best circumstances. Jeff was much happier working with their aunt's carpenter boyfriend than he had ever been at school, and Mom seemed more like her old self than she had in years. Between all that, and the support of her boyfriend Ethan, she had finally found some peace.

She was happy.

Now, all Todd wanted was to make sure she stayed that way. Feeling safe. Secure. And making sure the clinic was successful without her having to be there every day or worry about it was a big part of that.

Todd rolled down his window, letting the crisp afternoon air clear his head. It was good to get away from the clinic, even if it was for more work. An Alice Neilson had scheduled an appointment online using the new system he'd set up, requesting a house call for her pet named Barnaby. It had only launched the day before, and he was still working out the kinks on the request form.

First on the list?

Adding a field for "pet type".

"Dummy," he murmured, letting out a rueful chuckle.

That's what he got for trying to write code at 1 AM after a long day of work.

One field he hadn't forgotten to include, though, was a section for notes. That was where Alice Nielson had mentioned she couldn't even get close to Barnaby, much less coax him into a cage that would fit in her car.

That narrowed the options down a little, although not by much. He likely wasn't going to be walking in on a Great Dane or Burmese Mountain Dog, but most everything else was still on the table.

He was guessing semi-feral cat. Wouldn't be his first tango with one of those. In fact, he kind of hoped it was. He considered himself something of a Cat Whisperer. They liked him, probably because they sensed that he liked them. If it was a cat, he'd be good.

If it was a Chihuahua, though? He might be in trouble. He'd had a bad run of luck with them recently, and was starting to get a complex about it.

Todd heaved another sigh as he pulled up in front of an old cottage, double-checking the address against his GPS. It was a sweet little house with white paint and blue shutters, but as he walked up the pathway, the peaceful air was shattered.

"Miserable old fart!" croaked an old lady.

Todd jerked to a stop, staring up at the blue front door.

"Stop that! It's so rude!" another female voice shouted back.

He trudged up the steps and rapped on the door, wondering what the hell he was walking into. His knock went unheeded, and the shouting inside continued.

"Let's make a deal," the old woman squawked.

"I'm not making any deals with you until you stop trying to kill me!"

Todd drew back and then banged on the door harder. "Ms. Nielson?" he called loudly. "It's Dr. Ketterman."

The voices went silent and then he heard footfalls. The door opened a moment later and he blinked in surprise. Huge, hopeless, so-dark-they-were-almost-black eyes stared out at him from a face far too young to be the source of all the screaming. The woman's forehead was creased in consternation, and a bandana on her head only half contained her mass of curly black hair. There was a streak of dirt on her nose, and her oversized clothes were covered in dust.

She looked like the most beautiful hobo he'd ever laid eyes on.

"Thank God," she muttered, slumping against the doorjamb and blowing out a sigh.

"Is everything okay?" He tried for his best professional smile, but it felt strained as he tried to see past her into the house. "Are you in danger?"

She let out a snort. "Definitely."

There was a loud crash behind her and she flinched.

"He's a menace."

"Who?" he asked cautiously.

"Barnaby. The parrot." She whispered it, like she was

afraid if she said it too loud, she might summon him closer. "Sorry, I'm Alice. I guess... you should come in?"

"I guess so," Todd said with equal reluctance. He was glad she wasn't stuck in the house with a murderer, but her appearance led him to believe her actual situation wasn't a whole lot better.

That parrot must be a real handful.

But thoughts of Barnaby fled as Alice stepped back to let him enter. He was the least of her problems, and Todd made a snap decision to take the home visit option off the website, ASAP. The place was the stuff of nightmares. A wall of musty, old books and boxes piled from floor to ceiling down the entryway and beyond, with just a person-sized pathway carved into. The dust in the air was so thick, everything looked hazy.

He sneezed.

"Gesundheit!" a voice squawked.

"What he said," Alice murmured, brown eyes wide. "Um, yeah. So this is the place. Let me just show you what I'm dealing with, here."

She led the way, moving gingerly around newspapers and magazines that were piled almost to the ceiling. The furniture was completely covered by junk. Piles of mail, old cookie tins, glass bottles... It was straight from that show his ex used to binge-watch in college, *Hoarders*. It had been hard enough to see it on the screen. Being in the middle of it, though? Was a whole other thing.

How had such a young woman amassed such a collection of junk?

Todd peered at Alice through the gloom. He had never seen her in town; he would have remembered a face like hers.

She was gorgeous, despite the sweat and grime. Black, corkscrew curls, high cheekbones, full, soft-looking lips.

"Come on down!" the voice shrieked, jerking him from his reverie.

Alice winced.

How could anyone even think in this mess? He'd been here two minutes and already his thoughts were as cluttered as the living room.

"Barnaby's cage is in the kitchen," Alice said apologetically. "I would have used the back door, but I can't get to it right now..."

"You big dummy!" the parrot squawked. It did sound eerily similar to an old lady. One who had smoked a couple packs a day. Todd noted the cartons piled against one wall and the smell of mildew layered on top of dust and cooking grease.

And bird poop, he added with a wince.

Let's not forget the bird poop.

Ancient droppings crusted nearly every surface.

The kitchen, once they found it, was slightly less cluttered. One wall was taken up by a massive cage, where a great green macaw was giving them the side eye. Most of his plumage was a deep shade of chartreuse, with vibrant blue wing feathers and a bright red patch above his lethal-looking, black beak. He was a gorgeous animal and Todd said as much to Alice as the bird watched them in silence.

"Yeah, he's real pretty to look at, but the noise is hellacious. He mostly talks when no one is looking at him," Alice added quickly. "And it's almost exclusively quotes from old TV programs and gameshows. When I'm in the kitchen, though, he just stares at me with those beady little eyes."

Barnaby shifted his weight from foot to foot as he surveyed them.

"He looked healthy enough a week ago," Alice continued miserably. "I've been giving him his same food and everything. He barely touched it, though, and I was worried that he was getting sick. Then his feathers started falling out. What do you think is wrong with him?"

Barnaby paced uneasily in his cage, and Todd spotted a bare patch on the left side of his body.

"I don't think they're falling out," Todd said grimly. "I'm going to guess he's pulling them out." Todd moved slowly towards the cage and spoke in a soft, low voice as he examined the macaw.

"What?" Alice's winged, black brows flew high in alarm. "Why would he do that?"

"Stress, maybe? Depression," Todd said, shaking his head. "Macaws are social animals. They're intelligent. Maybe he needs some toys, or a friend—"

"I want to be his friend, but he hates me! And I feel awful because he's stuck in that stupid cage all the time..." Tears welled in Alice's eyes. "I can barely feed him without him biting me." She held out one bandaged hand as evidence.

"You used to let him out," Todd said gently, "what's changed?"

"Oh, no way. Mmm-mm. I never let him out," Alice insisted, shaking her head furiously. "He'd probably pluck my eyeballs out with those talons and eat them."

He glanced pointedly at a mound of bird turd just inches away on the countertop.

Alice followed his gaze and then looked back at him in stunned horror as she took a step back.

17

"I don't—" she began, looking mortified as she held a hand to her chest. "You don't think I live here? Oh my God, Dr. Ketterman, I don't live here! This is my great auntie's house."

A sense of relief rolled over him, and he let out a long breath. That explained so much.

"I've been coming here the past week, trying to sort through all of this," Alice continued as she shoved a towering pile of magazines to the floor and sank into an old, wooden chair. "I've hauled away at least fifty bags of trash, but I can't even tell the difference. It's never-ending. I'm buried alive under stacks of magazines from the fifties about what a good wife should do to make her husband happy, while a vicious parrot squawks TV catchphrases at me. Pretty sure that was how Dante described the fourth ring of hell."

"I'm so sorry," Todd said, wishing he knew what else to say. There was no point trying to tell her it wasn't that bad. It *was* that bad. In fact, he couldn't wait to leave and take a shower, and he hadn't even been trying to clean the place. "You deserve a medal. And a trophy. And maybe a key to the city for this," he said, gingerly setting his bag down onto a pile of boxes after finding a spot that was clear of little, ashy landmines of bird poop.

A quiet sob pulled Todd's gaze back to Alice. Her face was in her hands, and her shoulders shook beneath the fabric of her oversized t-shirt. Todd excavated a second chair from the rubbish and sat facing her. He wished he had taken Pop's advice and kept a handkerchief handy for just these types of occasions, but he had nothing to offer. Alice wiped her nose and face on the hem of her shirt.

"I'm so sorry. I'm a mess," she said miserably. "I can't do this."

"Do you want to sit outside and talk about it?" he asked, empathy welling inside him as he considered her circumstances.

"Yes," Alice said emphatically.

She stood and began to navigate the towers of rubbish, and Todd followed. Outside, they each took a deep breath before sitting down on the porch steps. The bright afternoon sunlight paired with the crisp autumn air felt awesome. When was the last time he had just sat outside in the sun?

"It smells so good out here. So clean," Alice murmured, eyes on the clear blue sky. Todd realized that he was staring. Even streaked with sweat and grime, her face was so lovely. He cleared his throat and turned his gaze toward the overgrown bushes out front.

"I don't know what to do with Barnaby," Alice said at last. "My great Auntie Louise loves him so much, but she broke her hip when she tripped on a pile of newspapers. She's been moved from the hospital to a rehabilitation facility until she can walk on her own again. My uncle, her son, is trying to find a home that will let her bring him — she can't come back here. She can't be alone all day every day, and can't afford daily help to come in. But so far he hasn't found a retirement home she can afford that will let her bring a giant parrot."

Her eyes were still red from crying. Out in the sunlight, they weren't so dark. More of a glass-bottle brown, luminous...

Alice turned her gaze back to the open sky. "Anyway, Auntie Louise is an amazing woman. She spent all the family holidays with us when I was growing up...every so often she would even bring Barnaby. He was less ornery when he was younger. I used to love watching her with him. She was really good to him. She was also a lot of fun to be around. She and Grandpa would get into these good-natured arguments, and we would all just watch them and laugh. I don't know, it sounds weird when I try to explain it. It was like... going to a debate, except they were funny.

"She worked at a pie shop, and so that was always her contribution. She would bring huge stacks, more than we could eat. Pumpkin and apple and berry crumble..." Tears welled in Alice's eyes. "I hadn't seen her in years. I was busy with school on the other side of the country, and I didn't always make it home for holidays anymore. Even when I did, she wasn't there..." Her voice trailed off. "I never really thought about why we never went to her house. I only found out it was like this when my uncle asked if I could help out. Get the place ready for showings so she could sell it, and take care of Barnaby in the meantime."

"I'm guessing you didn't know the extent of it," he said softly.

"Lord, no. I don't think it was this bad before her husband passed." A laugh bubbled from her lips. "I had a realtor meet me here the day I got into town so she could give us an assessment and let us know what needed doing. You should've seen her face," she added, still chuckling. "She walked in, turned on her heel and walked right back out. She said, 'Call me when we can even see if the floors are hardwood'."

A string of obscenities poured through a nearby open window, and Alice groaned.

"Sorry. Auntie Louise mostly watched TV Land and old shows, but she also had a thing for Robert DeNiro movies."

"I'm okay. He's just mimicking what he hears, so don't worry about me. I'm more worried about you. You've got a Herculean task ahead of you," Todd said, gesturing to the closed door behind them.

"Well, Barnaby's not exactly a Stymphalian bird, but yeah, pretty much."

Todd found himself grinning as he cocked his head. "A what?"

Alice glanced at him with a shrug. "A Stymphalian bird. You know, the birds that Hercules had to defeat for his... I think it was the sixth of the twelve labors. They were man eaters with bronze beaks and razor-sharp metal feathers that they could launch like projectiles."

Her face lit up as she spoke, and Todd realized that he was staring again. This time, he didn't look away.

Alice laughed - a light, musical sound - and said, "They even had toxic dung. The birds belonged to Ares, the god of war. They had taken over this swath of the countryside, destroying crops, killing townspeople. So Hercules scared them off with a rattle."

"A rattle," Todd repeated, deadpan.

Alice nodded. "Athena gave it to him. It was made by Hephaestus. He was the god of blacksmiths, metallurgy, all of that. Anyway, the rattle scared them away. Hercules shot a few for good measure."

"I'm impressed."

"Useless knowledge," Alice said, a cloud passing over her face. "That's why I offered to help. English degree I haven't been able to figure out how to use, lots of jobs but no career,

21

so I wasn't leaving behind much. My brother and sister have families and heavy work commitments. I can work anywhere."

"Starving artist?" Todd said, keeping his tone light.

"Not quite starving, but not living the dream, either. I play music sometimes, coffee shops and the like. I also write articles and content for websites. Sometimes I even get paid to write something that matters. That's why I'm stuck here. I'm the only one in the family who can work from anywhere, so I volunteered to go get Auntie's house ready to sell. I had no idea what I was signing up for. I thought I could stay in the cottage, take care of her bird, walk to the beach...write things that I care about. There's this writers' retreat this summer at Lake Squamish—"

Suddenly, Alice sat up straight.

"Man, I'm so sorry, Dr. Ketterman. You came for a house call and then I pulled you into this mess."

"You can call me Todd," he said. Alice held his gaze for a long moment and then nodded.

"Well, I'm sorry for talking your ear off, Todd."

He pulled playfully at one of his ears, and then the other. "Still firmly attached."

"I think I'm just sort of losing it a little. I haven't talked to anyone but Barnaby in days," Alice admitted. "Even when I'm at my rental, I'm mostly just writing. It all just spilled out. Forgive me."

"Please stop apologizing," Todd said earnestly. "I really don't mind. In fact, I wish I could stay longer." He glanced at his watch and realized the time with a start. "But I have a surgery in ninety minutes and—" he cleared his throat, not wanting to make her feel worse by telling her he had to stop home to shower, "I've got some paperwork to do beforehand. Don't think I'm giving up on you, though. Or Barnaby, rather. Typically, when birds bite, it's not because they're aggressive. It's a sign of stress. He's probably scared and missing your aunt. The feather picking is a bad sign. If birds get really anxious, they'll sometimes go beyond that and start chewing their own skin. We want to nip this in the bud before then. Let's do this," he said, rising to stand, and swiping the dirt off his pants as she joined him. "Once I'm done at the clinic today, I'll do some research. I don't know all that much about macaws in particular, but I'm sure I'll be able to come up with something that will help. We'll call it a continuation of today's home visit, on the house. Give me a day or so, and try to hang in there in the meantime, all right?"

She nodded, looking relieved and even a little hopeful. "I hate to keep making you come back. I'm sure you're very busy."

"You're not making me do anything. It's my job."

How he would carve out the time to do it, he had no freaking clue. But as he looked down at the woman on the steps beside him, he realized he didn't care. He was going to figure out a way to help her and that mouthy bird.

If he could do it without getting his eyeballs plucked out and eaten?

Well, even better.

NIKKI

"So MUCH FOR a relaxing day at the spa," Mateo said, brows raised in surprise as she finished relaying the story to him. "What even made Beth decide to come to town?"

"She saw the newspaper article," Nikki replied, shoving the last of her clothes into her already stuffed suitcase. "About Steve's suicide."

"Oh, Nikki," Mateo murmured. "I'm so sorry she had to find out that way. Come here." He walked over and wrapped his strong arms around her.

Nikki stood stiff for a moment. Beth was waiting for her in the Airbnb they'd found, and Nikki had an inventory running in her head of everything she needed to pack. She still had to grab her stuff from the bathroom... she could come back for her pots and pans... Would it be better to have a simple Thanksgiving meal just her and Beth, not intrude on a Sullivan family Thanksgiving? Should she convince Beth that they should head to Cherry Blossom Point, instead? Dad and Lena had so been looking forward to seeing her—

"I can hear your thoughts churning from here. Just let it

go for a second and take a breath," Mateo said softly against her hair.

She let out a long sigh and allowed herself to melt into Mateo's strong chest.

"It's just a lot, that's all."

"I know. It'll be okay, though," Mateo reassured her. "She's had a shock, but she'll rally and likely be stronger for it. Nineteen is a rough age. They want to be so independent, but they're still so dependent. Living on her own and playing grown up, but still a kid in so many ways. There's push and pull even when there isn't something traumatic going on."

Nikki pulled back to look up into Mateo's eyes. "I feel like I failed her."

"You didn't," he said, and kissed her forehead. "You know you didn't. She was upset, and she ran to you. She could have run off, or stayed put and shut you out. But instead she came and found you. That says a lot about her, and about your relationship. You've done good."

Nikki's shoulders slumped and she sat down on the bed. Mateo sat next to her, wrapping an arm around her, and she leaned into him.

"She wants to stay in Bluebird Bay for Thanksgiving. Get to know Anna."

Mateo gave her hip a squeeze. "That's great."

"I guess. It doesn't feel great. I feel overwhelmed."

"It's not Thanksgiving yet," Mateo said. He rubbed her arm in a reassuring way that brought all the scattered bits of Nikki's attention back to center. "You have time to reconnect. She can let all this gel in her mind and you two can cozy up and watch movies. Take her to walk the beach in the middle of the day when it's not so cold. Heck, take her to the bowling alley."

Nikki chuckled, picturing ten-year-old Beth in bowling shoes, holding a bright pink ball. It had been *the* thing when Beth was in fifth grade, a seemingly endless string of bowling-alley birthday parties. And then she'd blinked, and Beth was eighteen, running up the steps of her college dorm.

"I'm glad that you'll both be here a while longer," Mateo continued. "I know you'll need some time at home, but I'd love the chance to meet her. If not now, maybe toward Christmas time when you're back home?"

"I'd like that," Nikki replied. "I want her to get to know you. I don't know if it will happen on this visit, but soon, for sure."

"I understand," he assured her.

"And I'd like to meet Tara sometime, too."

Mateo's daughter Tara lived in Connecticut; she was in her last year of school at UConn on a basketball scholarship. She had a feeling that Beth would get on great with Mateo's daughter, too. From pictures and everything Mateo had said about her, she seemed to be funny, easygoing, and an all-around great kid. It made sense. Mateo was a great guy, and the kind of man that Nikki wished she could have given Beth as a father.

"Maybe the four of us can get together sometime," Mateo suggested. "Tara's always down for a getaway. A long weekend in the Adirondacks? Or a longer trip this summer. We'll see how things play out, but no pressure."

Nikki felt a small thrill go through her body at the mention of summer. They hadn't even tried the long distance thing yet, and she felt touched that Mateo had so much confidence in them. Or if not confidence, at least hope. She felt hopeful, too, more than she had in a long while.

Nikki leaned on Mateo for a minute longer, letting that hope warm her, and then she stood.

"I will definitely think about it. I've got to go, though. I don't want to leave Beth waiting too long."

"Of course," Mateo agreed. He lifted her heavy suitcase with ease. "I'll put this in your car while you do a final sweep. Or," he added with a wink, "if you wanted to 'forget' something here, and come back for it, that would be okay, too."

He walked out and Nikki gathered her things from the bathroom, tossing bottles and brushes into a single bag. When she came out, Mateo was waiting by the front door.

"I've loved having you here, Nikki. I'll miss you. Call when you can."

"Don't worry," Nikki told him with a nervous laugh. "You'll probably get tired of my texts. I'll need to vent, and I'll need your sage advice on managing a nineteen-year-old daughter."

Mateo kissed her, a quick peck on the lips. "You know her better than anyone, Nikki. Everything will turn out fine."

Nikki pulled him back in and kissed him again. For one long moment, her head was clear of worry. Then, Mateo straightened up and smiled at her.

"I'll see you soon," he told her in a voice filled with promise. "Call anytime. Text as often as you'd like. I promise I won't get tired of them."

The days ahead might not be easy, Nikki reflected as she climbed into her car, but at least she had some support here in Bluebird Bay. After the ongoing nightmare that was her ex-husband, and then her long years as a single mother, Nikki had written off the idea of ever finding a good man. She shook her head in awe as she drove down the road.

Mateo was everything she had never dared to hope for. Strong, gentle, kind... *gorgeous,* a little voice in her head added. He was generous and helpful, going out of his way to make sure that Nikki felt safe.

And the best part?

He liked her enough that he planned to drive two hours to Cherry Blossom Point just to see her. Steve had been her entire life for years, and then it was all about being with and protecting Beth. Now that she was grown, Beth was still a bright light for Nikki, but she had her own life now. Sure, she needed her mom for the next week or so, but after that, it was back to school, and Nikki would only hear from her once every week or two via text. It was nice to have her relationship with Mateo on the horizon, like a sweet promise waiting.

And then there was Anna, who had been a real rock since everything that had happened with Steve. She was doubly blessed in Bluebird Bay, and it was truly starting to feel like a second home to her.

Nikki stopped for groceries on her way across town and then found the apartment building where she was meeting her daughter. She walked up to the third floor, where the door to apartment 304 was unlocked. Beth sat on the couch watching something Nikki didn't recognize.

"Hi, honey," she said brightly. "I stopped for supplies. Everything we need to make Monster Mac."

Nikki's green mac and cheese had been Beth's favorite food for years, and she'd told her mom how much she missed it now that she was stuck eating most of her meals at the campus cafeteria. But now Beth barely spared her a glance.

"Cool," she said, eyes back on the TV. "Thanks."

Nikki went and put the milk and cheese in the fridge, then went to join Beth on the couch. Beth paused her show, but still wouldn't look her in the eyes.

"I've missed you," Nikki told her.

Beth was silent, looking down at the fuzzy blanket she'd pulled over her legs. For a moment, Nikki had one of those flashes, when the young woman in front of her seemed to occupy the same space as the little girl with the gap-toothed grin who had been her whole world.

When had things gotten so jumbled? They needed a clean slate.

"Do you have any questions for me?" Nikki asked. "No more secrets. I promise."

"It's really weird," Beth said slowly. "I thought I wanted to know it all, and then, when I think of what you might say, and I think of Grandpa and Grammy, I keep thinking maybe I *don't* want to know."

"I get that." Nikki felt a wave of compassion for her daughter. "Aunt Gayle and Uncle Jack didn't even want to meet Anna. They wanted to pretend she didn't exist. It's understandable."

"I *wanted* to meet her," Beth said. "I just feel really confused now."

"Also understandable," Nikki replied. "Let's just be together for now, huh? We don't need to make any big decisions today. Will you help me with the Monster Mac?"

"Sure."

They worked together in companionable silence, falling

29

back into a comfortable rhythm they had developed over the years. Beth shredded cheese while Nikki boiled pasta and chopped onions. She caramelized them slowly, adding jalapeño peppers and thyme. Then she started the cheese sauce while Beth filled a blender with spinach and arugula. When the pasta was done, Beth added some of the starchy pasta water to the blender. She turned it on and added the resulting puree to the white cheese sauce, turning it the vibrant shade of green that had delighted her as a kid.

"Mom?" Beth said as she poured the cheese sauce over the pasta. "Do you think my dad was broken inside?"

Nikki froze, caught off guard by the question.

"Like, was he born bad or...?"

"Oh, Beth." Nikki took a deep breath and tried to gather her thoughts. Steve had been a narcissistic, controlling psychopath. He'd only cared about Nikki because of the way she made him feel. Correction: The way he'd *made* her make him feel. Like the center of the universe. He loved himself far too much to spare any for his daughter. If anything, he had resented her as a baby for consuming Nikki's attention... and finally inspiring her mother to gather her courage to leave him. But the truth was, she had no idea who Steve would've been if he'd had a good life growing up.

"I do think he was broken," Nikki said slowly. "He had such a terrible childhood, Beth. His parents were abusive, and it wasn't until his older brother wound up in a coma that they all went into foster care. Steve never found a permanent home. His brother never made it out of the hospital, and his older sister got hooked on heavy drugs. Steve just bounced around the rest of his childhood, and he was on his own at eighteen.

"Some people manage to heal from a childhood like that. I don't know how... or why some people are able to be good parents even after a terrible childhood, while others never manage to climb out of that pit. But no, I don't think he was born bad. He just didn't know how to break away and stop the cycle of abuse. So I did it for him. For us. We broke that cycle."

Beth nodded, and blew out a heavy sigh. "Thanks for telling me the truth. I really needed to hear it. I'm going to go wash up for dinner." She excused herself and ducked into the bathroom.

Nikki put their pasta into the oven to bake and then slumped into a chair. Her daughter seemed less angry, but it was even harder on Nikki's heart to see Beth so sad and confused.

Her thoughts were derailed when her phone buzzed and she picked it up, expecting a *How's it going?* text from Mateo. Instead, she saw it was a voicemail from her sister Lena.

Her stomach sank. If she planned to stay in Bluebird Bay for Thanksgiving, she still needed to call Lena and the others to tell them that she and Beth wouldn't be coming home...

Or maybe she would just call her dad, and then send a group text to the rest of them, and silence the replies. Lena would be disappointed that they were missing the holiday, but Jack and Gayle? Would be livid. And, frankly, she just didn't have the mental or emotional bandwidth to deal with them right now. Nikki was more than willing to drop everything for her daughter, but she didn't have the energy to coddle grown adults. She was still working to process the events of the past month herself. Tonight, she just needed a break.

She dropped the phone into her purse, vowing to deal with it all tomorrow. A moment later, Beth came out of the bathroom, eyes a telltale shade of pink that pulled at Nikki's heart.

"It feels like a *Gilmore Girls* kind of night," Nikki said, naming the show that they had watched together in its entirety when Beth was in high school. Light, funny, and full of cute, mother-daughter banter. "Sound good?"

Beth's face brightened, and she seemed relieved to have a break from the weight of the day. "Yeah. That sounds good."

They ate the entire pan of mac and cheese, watching episode after episode, chatting and laughing at parts. Hours later, Beth fell asleep on the couch. Nikki tucked her in and just watched her for a while, like she'd done when Beth was little and Nikki had lost sleep to the irrational fear that her daughter would simply stop breathing one night. Beth's cheeks were still childishly round. She looked so young, asleep in the light of the TV. So peaceful.

Nikki turned the television off and crossed the living room to stand at the window. She could see a sliver of ocean between two buildings. Moonlight glinted off of the water as waves crashed against the shore.

Whatever she had to do to make that peace a reality for her daughter over the next week, she was going to do it. And if that meant tuning her older siblings out, so be it. The time would come to pay the piper. Unless a genie came to pay her a visit, she'd have to deal with Jack and Gayle eventually.

But not today.

4

CEE-CEE

THE BELL above the door of Cee-cee's Cupcakes jangled and Cee-cee looked up with a welcoming smile, which only widened when she saw who walked in. Max looked bright and cheerful, and it did Cee-cee's heart good to see her looking so well. Their family had been through the wringer these past two years, and Max had seen her share of stress and heartache. But her bookshop was thriving against all odds, and she seemed blissfully happy with her new boyfriend. Both of Cee-cee's children were content, and all was well in her world.

Of course, with a family as large and close-knit as theirs, there was always a tremor somewhere in the web. Anna had another surprise relative in town, but she seemed to be dealing with her new niece much more easily than she had with her sister Nikki. With no children of her own, Anna seemed eager to soak up time with her boyfriend's grandson, Teddy, and now with her new niece, Beth.

Cee-cee's son Gabe and his wife Sasha had gotten off to a rough start, but they seemed to be doing well, now. Cee-cee was so excited to meet her first grandchild, even if the thought of her baby boy becoming a father still made her head spin sometimes.

But then there was Nate. While Cee-cee had no love for her ex-husband, he was still the father of her children. As such, she cared about what happened to him. And he hadn't been himself for a long time... not since their divorce, now that she thought of it. Probably before that, but it had happened so slowly that she hadn't noticed. Of course, he hadn't wanted her to notice...

"I'm sooo hungry," Max said, breaking Cee-cee's train of thought. "What have you got for me?"

"Today's batch of Lemony Snickets are still in the oven," Cee-cee replied. "But I always have something for you. Orange Creamsicle?"

"Cupcakes for breakfast?" Max grinned. "Sure. Thanks, Mom. Is there coffee?"

"Always," she told her daughter. "You grab two mugs. I'll get the cupcakes."

Cee-cee plated two newly frosted cakes as well as a pair of chocolate mini-muffins, and went to her favorite table, the one with the best ocean view. Max joined her, and they clinked their mugs together in wordless cheers.

Max took a sip of her coffee and sighed contentedly. "This is nice. Ian usually makes breakfast, but he left for work at dawn today. Some kid broke one of his puzzles yesterday, trying to figure out the Alice-themed room. He went in to fix it before his first booking today."

"It sounds like his business is doing well."

"Really well," Max said with a grin. She picked up her cupcake and Cee-cee watched anxiously while she bit into it.

"How is it?" she asked.

Max frowned at her. "What do you mean? Everyone loves your orange-vanilla cupcakes. Did you change something?"

A wave of excitement swept over Cee-cee, and she grinned. "It's gluten free."

"What?" Max's nose crinkled. "Why?"

Cee-cee laughed. "I get customers asking for gluten-free cupcakes every. Single. Day. Not just the tourists, either. Patricia Kimble is desperate to have her daughter's birthday here, but her little girl can't eat wheat without getting sick."

"Yeah, people ask for gluten-free muffins at the bookshop, too," Max acknowledged.

"I'm going to have a dedicated case and everything," Cee-cee told her. "I think our sales will go up a lot. I'll have to charge more for them because of the cost of the ingredients, but I think people expect that. I've been working on recipes for weeks, trying to figure out a blend of flours that would work. Most of the combinations I tried lacked something in the texture department, but I think I finally figured it out."

Max had already finished her cupcake.

"It's really good, Mom. I truly couldn't tell the difference."

"Adding cassava and coconut flour to the mix made all the difference," Cee-cee said with satisfaction. "I have it all written down. Now, I can just mix up big batches of my own blend ahead of time." She took a bite of her own cupcake and nodded in satisfaction. She could still tell the difference between this version and the original, but they were equally delicious.

Max helped herself to one of the chocolate mini-muffins and leaned back in her seat.

"This is really good, too," she said after her first bite. "Kind of... floral?"

"I went easy on the chocolate and added rosewater. You like it?"

"Awesome." Max nodded emphatically. "Oh! I forgot to ask you! How was your sisters' spa day, anyway?" she asked around a mouthful of muffin.

"Relaxing," Cee-cee said slowly. "At first."

Max slumped back in her seat and swallowed. "Uh oh. Now what?"

"We had a surprise visit from Beth."

"Beth?" Max said blankly, and then her eyebrows shot up. "Nikki's Beth?"

"The very same," Cee-cee confirmed.

"What's she like?"

"In that moment? Angry." Cee-cee shrugged. "We didn't get a chance to talk. But Anna texted me that they'll be in town for a few days. I want to invite them to Thanksgiving."

"What did Aunt Anna say?"

"She's all for it. She invited them to stay at her house, but they ended up at that cute little apartment complex across from the pier."

"Wow. She and Nikki have come a long way."

"They have," Cee-cee agreed.

"Do you want to see if she wants me to meet Beth? She might be open to talking to someone closer to her age."

"That's nice of you, sweetie. Let's put a pin in that for now. I think she and Nikki need some time alone together to process everything that's happened."

"Fair enough," Max said. They were silent for a moment, enjoying their sweets and the view.

"Have you heard from Dad?" Max asked with some hesitation.

"Now that you mention it, I'm meeting him for dinner tonight," Cee-cee replied carefully.

"Seriously?" Max asked, wide-eyed.

"Seriously. I told you that I would get to the bottom of this, and that's what I intend to do. If your dad is in trouble, I want to know what's going on before it gets any worse."

"Be discreet, Mom. You know how Dad shuts down when he feels cornered."

"I have thirty years of practice handling that man," Cee-cee said with a clipped nod. "I'll tread lightly."

"Okay." Max finished her coffee and cleared her place at the table while Cee-cee lingered, still eating her Orange Creamsicle cupcake. The frosting was better than ever now that she'd started making her own vanilla extract.

"These chocolate muffins are for the bookshop, right?"

"Like Rosewater for Chocolate," Cee-cee confirmed.

"Adorable name." Max boxed them up. "Thanks, Mom," she said, giving her a quick kiss on the cheek. "Keep me posted."

It was a bustling day at the cupcake shop and the time flew by so fast, Cee-cee barely had time to worry about her meet up with Nate. The new recipes sold like gluten-free hotcakes, with a sign on the sidewalk pulling in new customers like a siren song. Finally, Cee-cee slipped away to her apartment upstairs, leaving her trusty employees Pete and Wanda to handle closing and cleanup.

Now, though, freshly showered and away from the hustle

of the bakery, Cee-cee stood in front of her closet filled with a low-key sense of dread.

What clothes said, *"I'm here because you'll always be the father of my children and I care about you, but if you think that I'm even remotely interested in getting back together, you're out of your friggin' mind!"*?

She was tempted to wear one of her fiancé's flannel shirts, but in the end she threw on a comfortable pair of jeans and a sweater the color of red wine. Nate, ever the epitome of fashion and propriety, would probably hate that. Then again, what Nate liked was no longer her concern.

When she walked into Monzano's half an hour later, she spotted him at one of the far tables. He sat with his head down, shredding a paper napkin between his fingers.

Here we go.

She put her chin up and approached her ex with a smile.

Nate dropped the napkin and plastered a grin on his own face when he spotted her. His silver-streaked hair was neatly combed, and he wore a black, lightweight wool suit. He stood from his seat and pulled Cee-cee's chair out for her in a baffling show of chivalry.

Weird.

"It's good to see you," Nate said as he sank back into his chair. "You look amazing."

Cee-cee was tempted to say that just a couple years ago he would have given her a look of cold disdain for going out to a restaurant in a pair of jeans, but the appreciation in his eyes seemed genuine and there was no point in starting off on a bad foot.

"Thanks. Have you ordered yet?"

"Of course not, I was waiting for you." He waved to the

waiter approaching their table. "A bottle of your best cabernet, please."

Cee-cee met the waiter's eyes and gave him an apologetic smile.

"Let's put a pin in that. I'll need a minute to look at the menu."

"Of course," the young man said. He placed their menus on the table and moved on to the next guests.

Nate was frowning at her. "What was that about?"

"I was about to ask you the same thing," Cee-cee said. Might as well dive right in while she had the opening. "This isn't a date, and it isn't a business meeting. You don't have to impress me. What are you doing ordering a two-hundred-dollar bottle of wine when you're so desperate for investors that you had to trick Max's new boyfriend into a hard-sell business meeting under the guise of a friendly meal with her father?"

The color drained from Nate's face as she spoke. His eyes flicked around the room, avoiding her gaze.

"It wasn't like that. I already told Max I was sorry, it was a miscommunication. And you know me, I'm always looking for investment opportunities. It's hard to turn off sometimes."

Cee-cee snorted and blocked his face with her menu.

Sorry, Max, she thought, not even seeing the words in front of her face as she took a few deep, steadying breaths.

So much for treading lightly. She used to know exactly how to handle Nate—hell, she still did—but somehow, the thought of stroking his ego and buttering him up like she used to was both sickening and exhausting. She simply didn't have the patience for it anymore, and she didn't want to.

She'd have to find another way to skin this cat.

The waiter returned and Cee-cee ordered spaghetti aglio e olio with the house red. A simple plate of noodles and garlic sounded good. The garlic would serve as a warning sign for Nate to stay on his side of the table, and drowning her feelings in carbs would be like a warm hug. The old Cee-cee would have ordered a salad. How had she wasted so many years silently eating leaves while she listened to this man talk? She rolled her eyes as Nate ordered the veal and a fifteen dollar glass of cabernet.

Why was she even wasting an evening with him, when she could be cuddled up on the couch with Mick?

Max's concerned face flashed in her mind, and she sighed.

Right.

"So tell me...how are Gabe and Sasha getting on?" Nate asked as they waited for their food. "I spoke to him on the phone briefly last week, and he seemed good."

Cee-cee smiled in spite of herself. "Yeah. They seem great, actually. Although, who can say for sure. It's hard to know what's really going on in a marriage—" Nate frowned and Cee-cee rushed forward, "but I think they're doing really well. Max has been an amazing sister to the both of them. Sasha's really lonely for family, I think."

Nate flashed his most charming smile. "She has plenty of family now."

Cee-cee thanked the waiter as he brought their food, and slurped up a single long noodle before responding.

"I felt the baby kick last time I saw them. Grace. I can't wait to hold her. I bet she'll have a head full of black hair, just like Gabe did."

"Maybe," Nate said, sounding distracted as he cut into his veal. "Nice name."

Cee-cee sighed and took another bite of her food. At least that was engaging. Spaghetti aglio e olio was usually made with olive oil, but Monzano's added butter, too. The rich noodles were generously spiced with fresh garlic and red pepper and she plugged another forkful into her mouth.

"It's so nice to share a meal with you after all this time," Nate said with a smile. "We should've done this sooner."

Cee-cee almost choked on her mouthful of pasta. She swallowed, and said lightly, "I don't know if you've heard the news, Nate, but this just in: Men who cheat on their wives of thirty years with their realtor and then dump them with a note don't normally get to drink fine wine over a meal with their exes."

The grin dropped from Nate's face and he hung his head with an expression of such profound hurt that Cee-cee immediately felt a prickle of guilt. Damn him for making *her* feel bad. She took a deep breath and set down her fork.

"I apologize. That was uncalled for. I was trying to make a joke, and clearly it fell flat. I don't have any animosity in my heart for you, Nate."

He shot her a skeptical look.

"I really don't. What you did — not how you did it, but having the courage to break the cycle of a thirty-year marriage because you weren't content — was the best thing for both of us." *At least, it was the best thing for me, even though I didn't know it at the time...* "I'm so much happier now."

"I can see that." Nate gave her a bittersweet smile that almost made him look human. "I'm glad Mick makes you happy. And I'm really glad the shop is doing so well."

"I want you to be happy, too, Nate. It's infuriating when you try to wine and dine me like a client." Or worse, a cheap date. "We've known each other too long for that." She held his gaze and pressed. "And too long to keep secrets from each other. Especially important ones that might affect the kids."

Nate said nothing, eyes on his food. Cee-cee took a deep breath.

"Just tell me this; Is something going on with your business?" she asked. "Or your health?"

Nate looked up at her in surprise and responded with a swift shake of his head. "No. No, I feel great. Fitter than ever."

Okay, so this nut is just not ready to crack, Cee-cee thought in frustration, stabbing at her pasta.

They finished their meal in relative silence, peppered with small talk. Normally, Cee-cee would be tempted to order a slice of Monzano's boozy tiramisu, but she turned down the waiter's offer of dessert. She just wanted to get home to Mick. Her mind was on a tiramisu cupcake at home snuggled up on the couch as Nate insisted on paying for dinner.

"Thank you for joining me," he said in a subdued voice. "Can I give you a ride home?"

"No," Cee-cee replied. "Thank you, though. I drove over."

She hesitated, wishing she knew what else to say to get Nate to open up and tell her what was going on with him. But maybe she couldn't be that person to him anymore. If she were struggling, she certainly wouldn't turn to her ex-husband for comfort or advice. She set her napkin on the table and stood, defeated.

42

"Thanks for the meal, Nate. Take care," she added with feeling.

"See you around, Celia," he replied, eyes on his wallet as he searched for the right credit card.

The meal hadn't been a success, besides the delicious pasta, but she'd learned one thing for sure. Nate was definitely keeping something from her, Cee-cee reflected as she climbed into her car. She drove home on autopilot, still lost in thought as she parked and climbed the stairs to her apartment.

Tilly ran to greet her in a rush of furry affection and her mood instantly lifted. Cee-cee crouched down and ran a hand over her dog's soft coat, laughing as Tilly licked her face.

"We missed you," Mick said, drying his hands on a dish towel as he came around the corner.

Cee-cee stood and hugged him, breathing in the warm, woodsy scent of his flannel shirt. His arms wrapped around her. Not too tight or demanding. Not loose or distracted. His embrace was solid and comforting and wholly present.

Just right.

"How was dinner?" he asked softly.

Cee-cee surprised both of them by bursting into tears. She buried her face in his chest, feeling embarrassed.

"That bad, huh?" Mick asked as her tears subsided. "Come sit down on the couch and tell me about it."

Cee-cee nodded. "Just a minute." She went into the bathroom to blow her nose and splash cold water on her face. When she came out, Mick was waiting on the couch with two glasses of wine.

"Nothing happened," she told him as she sat down. "I

mean, we didn't fight or anything. He tried to schmooze me like he would a client, but he wouldn't tell me what's going on with him. He says he's excited to be a grandfather, but he wasn't even listening when I talked about Grace." Cee-cee shook her head, looking out at the moonlit waves. "I'm thinking I should tell Max that, until he's ready to talk, there isn't anything we can do. We've both got to let it go."

Even as she said the words, though, she knew she couldn't. For Max's mental well-being, she had to keep pressing.

Now, she just had to figure out how to get to the bottom of what the hell was going on with Nate...without asking Nate himself.

5

TODD

TODD HAD BROUGHT HOME MORE than his share of injured birds as a kid, and he'd seen a cockatiel or two at the clinic, but never a great green macaw. Even at Cornell, his experience with parrots had been limited to a two-week exotic species rotation at the university animal hospital. Luckily, there were shelves lined with books on every topic imaginable at the clinic. Mom had collected beginner's books over the years to loan to new pet owners, and she'd amassed quite a collection of complex medical texts. He'd spent the night before combing through the books and everything he could find on the internet, and was armed and ready for Barnaby as he headed back to the cottage that evening.

The bird books said that macaws were food motivated, so Todd had stopped on his way over and picked up a few different options. He had also purchased toys to hang in Barnaby's cage. An exasperated voice in the back of his mind told him that he didn't have the time or energy to be going to such lengths for a temporary, non-emergency patient. But he felt sorry for the stressed and grieving bird... and if he was being honest with himself, he felt just as sorry for Alice.

She seemed like a really good person in a bad situation.

Let's not forget how much you enjoyed her company, a little voice piped in.

That, too, he thought, blowing out a sigh. *But don't get used to it.*

He barely had enough time to squeeze a jog or a trip to the grocery store in some weeks.

"And yet, here we are," he muttered as he mounted the stairs.

This time, though, at least he had scheduled Barnaby as his last appointment of the day; he knew that gaining the macaw's trust would be a slow process.

Alice smiled at him as she opened the door. She was dressed in a garish Christmas sweater that hung down to her knees and faded blue jeans. Purplish shadows hung under her eyes. Inwardly, Todd marveled that she could look so beautiful even when she was so clearly exhausted.

She must have noted his glance at her clothes, because she shook her head. "I only wear what I'm willing to burn," she said with a chuckle. "I wondered if you'd be brave enough to come back."

"Yes, ma'am. The cavalry has arrived," said Todd with a grin, holding up the bags from the pet store.

"What is all that?"

"Tools of the trade," he said easily. "I can't approach that bird empty-handed."

"You didn't have to do that! It will take a miracle to get near him at all," Alice said over her shoulder as she led him through her aunt's maze of newspapers and boxes. "I've been having nightmares about Barnaby swooping down and tearing at my hair with his talons. Then that black beak comes for some soft tissue and I wake up. I didn't even sleep last night, but I did get Auntie's bedroom mostly cleared out. We're trying to gather up some of her things for when she's ready to transfer from the hospital to a home, so I figured I'd start there."

The maze spat them out into the kitchen, which was now more than halfway cleared of debris.

"You've made progress in here," Todd said, nodding in approval. "Good job."

Alice responded with a tired shrug. "Slowly but surely. I can only fit so many bags of trash in my car at one time, and the guys at the dump are surely sick of me, so I've ordered a dumpster to come this weekend. I can *almost* see the floor in the bedroom. Thing is, though, the more I get past the trash, the more stuff I'm finding. Lots of vinyl records, and amazing old books. The records, I'll keep, but the rest...I'm having to take some time sorting through it all because I can't bring myself to just sweep it into a bag. I don't even know what I'm going to do with it all. My mom surely wouldn't be happy if I brought it to her house."

"My cousin Max owns a bookstore just down the street. I bet she'd love to sort through the books."

Alice's exhaustion disappeared beneath the sunshine of her smile. "Do you really think she might be interested?"

"I don't see why not. When you've got them all together, I can call and see when a good time—" Todd began, cut short by an ear-splitting screech from Barnaby.

"Sorry. He's usually pretty quiet when there is someone in the room."

"Maybe he wants to get my attention." Todd moved towards the bird, bags held out before him like a peace offering. "Hey, Barnaby, old boy," he said softly.

Too late, he remembered the book's advice *not* to respond to shrieks. Oh well. He would work on gaining the macaw's trust, first. Getting him healthy, and to get him to stop biting; that had to come before addressing any other problem behaviors.

"I come bearing gifts."

Barnaby moved to the front of the cage, eying the bags with suspicion.

"I brought you a piñata," Todd said in a quiet, cheerful voice.

Behind him, Alice asked with a laugh, "A *what?*"

"A palm-leaf piñata," Todd whispered as he cautiously unlocked the door of the cage.

Barnaby growled.

"I wouldn't—" Alice tried to warn him as he put his hand into the cage to grab the empty food bowl. Barnaby lunged for him with his beak, but Todd was prepared for that. He steeled himself, and didn't even flinch as Barnaby bit him.

Todd's gamble paid off. It had been a test bite, not a vicious attack. Barnaby eyed him with curiosity, obviously surprised that Todd hadn't shouted or jumped back.

"There's no need for that," said Todd in a soothing tone. "I'm not trying to hurt you..." He slowly inserted the piñata into Barnaby's cage and clipped it to one of the bars on top. "Don't worry if he shreds it. He's supposed to. It's just to give him something to do, exercise his muscles and his mind."

Barnaby eyed it skeptically, but he didn't try to bite again.

"Progress," he said under his breath as he closed the door.

"Here's his food," Alice said, handing over a bag of nuts and dried fruit.

"Thanks." Todd filled the bowl, and then reached into the second bag. "Parrots like fresh food, too. I brought a few things to try. Can I borrow a knife?"

"Of course." Alice rummaged around until she found a paring knife.

Todd cut a few slices of apple and pear and put them on top of the dry food mix. He looked Barnaby in the eye as he approached the cage.

"No more biting," he said firmly. "I am the bringer of gifts."

Barnaby made no move to attack as Todd placed the food in his cage and closed the door.

"Progress," Alice agreed. She was smiling again, and Todd began to pull the rest of his offerings out of their shopping bags. "As upset as he was with Auntie Louise gone, I didn't want to shake up his routine even more by giving him people food."

"I get the thought process, but I think it will do him good. If you're eating fruit, you can offer to Barnaby. Slip it through the bars if you're afraid of getting bit, and we can work on that aggressive behavior over time."

Over time? What the hell was that? He didn't *have* any time, except the scant hours he managed to hoard over the weekend when the clinic was only open in the mornings for emergencies. Besides, she hadn't asked him to be her permanent avian consultant or something.

He cleared his throat and pushed on to cover his flub,

CHRISTINE GAEL

"The experts say that birds pick up on our emotions. If we're scared or unhappy when we approach them, they're more likely to bite. Same if you try to shoo them away."

"That explains it, then," she said with a curt nod. "I was definitely unhappy when I approached him the first time. I had just walked into this," she paused to gesture around the room, "and he was swearing at me. Not exactly the red carpet welcome. It was a shock, because Auntie Louise said he was such a love bug with her."

"He probably was, and now he's lost without her. So we've got to cheer him up. I bought a target stick — that's a training tool — and some treats. We can maybe start with those next time. I don't want to push him too far; if he's overwhelmed he'll start biting again. The feather plucking is a nervous behavior, but it also might just be boredom. Hopefully new toys will help; there are some more in here for after he shreds the piñata, or if he doesn't like it. There's also an herbal stress formula we can try, if he's still pulling feathers. I remember my mom gave it to one of her patients — a cockatoo — when there was construction noise going on next door and the bird—"

"Todd! You're bleeding!" Alice interrupted, eyes wide.

Todd glanced down at his hand in surprise. There was blood dripping from a small wound caused by Barnaby's warning bite, but it was nothing compared to some of the bites and scratches he'd gotten over the years.

"No biggie. Seriously, I'm good," he said, but Alice had already rushed out of the room. Todd put the fresh food into Louise's otherwise empty — and now clean – refrigerator, beside a bunch of water bottles. Then, he stood there awkwardly, waiting for Alice to come back. After a minute, she did, brandishing a canvas bag.

"I keep a first aid kit in my car. Let me see your hand."

Todd obliged, trying not to notice the scent of lemons that washed over him as she took his hand.

How could she possibly still smell so good after working here all day?

"So your mom's a vet too?" Alice asked as she wiped away the blood with an alcohol swab that stung a little. Her soft, musical voice made his pulse pound, but at the same time, he felt some of the constant stress of late melt away.

He cleared his throat before answering. "Yeah, she's the original Dr. Ketterman. She had a rough time of it after my dad died, so I've been slowly taking over at the clinic for her since I graduated."

"I'm sorry to hear about your dad," said Alice as she dabbed a smear of salve over the wound. "My dad passed away when I was twelve." Her eyes went wistful. "I still miss him a lot."

Man, he knew that feeling. "Me too." Todd squeezed her hand reflexively and her gaze shot to his. Suddenly, the room seemed a little too warm. He was about to say something, he wasn't sure what, when a sudden shriek split the air, and they jumped apart.

"Here's, uh, here's the Band-Aid," Alice said, holding out the little white packet, her cheeks flushed.

"Thanks," he replied.

They were both silent for a long moment as he peeled it open and covered the little puncture mark.

He tossed the empty packaging into a nearby garbage bag

and then turned his attention back to Barnaby. The bird had eaten every bit of the fresh fruit he'd left in the cage.

"Still hungry?" he asked mildly.

Barnaby bobbed his head up and down, ruffling the feathers on his neck as he studied Todd curiously.

"Okay then." Todd cut some more slices of pear and apple for the bird, and then looked Barnaby in the eye and said slowly, "We would really prefer it if you didn't scream."

"Kiss my grits," the parrot replied gravely.

Todd smothered a grin. "I'll take it."

He dropped the fruit in Barnaby's bowl and he instantly started devouring the apple slices.

"Vitamin A is good for him — there're some carrots and broccoli in the bag — and they usually like greens, too. You could give him baked yam or pumpkin. Even good, whole-grain bread or a little bit of yogurt. They need protein — they eat bugs in the wild." Todd racked his brain for the rest of what he'd read the night before. "But no chocolate, no avocado, no rhubarb. Some people even feed their macaws meat. They can eat rice and beans — cooked — and of course, nuts."

"Rice and beans, huh? Now you're talking."

"One of my favorites, too." He resisted the urge to mention Zapata's, the awesome Mexican place over by the pier, and how they should go sometime. *This is not an episode of The Bachelor. This is a house call for a parrot.*

"So," he said, clearing his throat, "where do you live when you're not acting as pet warden and house de-clutterer?" Todd asked casually.

"Portland. Born in Philadelphia, but my mom's from Maine, and she moved back here after I went to college. I think she wanted to move back as soon as my dad passed, but I'd been accepted to this fancy performing arts school, and she felt like it would be selfish to deprive me of the opportunity."

"You mentioned music last time, and I meant to ask. What do you play?" Todd asked, impressed.

Alice shrugged. "A few things. I started with the piano, and played cello for a minute. Mostly I played violin." She looked up at him, and a grin stole over her face. "Actually, what I really love is the fiddle."

"What's the difference?"

Alice laughed. "There isn't one. Well, some fiddles have five strings instead of four. And sometimes the bridge is flatter... but basically they're the same. It's the music that's different. Lively, folksy stuff instead of long-dead white guys. Don't get me wrong, I love it, too. But I want to play music to match my mood. They wouldn't let me play the fiddle in school. It was a stuffy place, all classical music. My mom wanted me to study music in college, but school took all the joy out of it. I studied English instead," she said with a bitter little laugh, "and let them take all the joy out of *that* instead. Nothing ruins a good book like a twenty-page essay."

"I'd like to hear you play sometime," Todd admitted gruffly. "The music you like to play."

"You're in luck!" Alice said, dark eyes glinting with banked pleasure. "Along with a bassoon, a tuba, three flutes, and a full drum set — none of which Auntie plays, as far as I know — I found a fiddle buried in all the junk. I was going to take it home last night, but the car was already so full of trash, I left it in the bedroom closet. I tuned it a bit, but I haven't really played it yet."

Alice disappeared and then reappeared a few minutes later holding a violin — *a fiddle,* Todd corrected himself immediately.

"Ready?" she asked with a grin. "Let's see what this thing can do."

She started off slow, pausing to make minute adjustments to the tuning, but before long her fingers were flying. Her boots tapped a rhythm on the linoleum floor as she played, and the bow rushed back and forth across the strings. It was dancing music, and Todd found his foot tapping along with hers.

When Alice finished her song, he was grinning from ear to ear.

"That was great."

"It's a good fiddle," she said. There was a new light in her eyes and color in her cheeks.

"What was that music?" Todd asked.

"My daddy was originally from Appalachia before we moved to the city," she said, affecting a heavy mountain accent, "and *his* daddy was a fiddle player." Dropping the twang, she continued, "I used to go there every summer, even after Daddy died. My grandparents lived up in the mountains, and it's a lot nicer than Philly in the summertime. My cousins and I would run wild all day, exploring the woods and the creek, and at night Grandpa would play the fiddle." Her eyes had a faraway look to them, until suddenly she snapped back to the present. "I'll put this away. Be right back."

You don't have time for a girlfriend, Todd reminded himself.

She doesn't even live here.

She's a client.

You're being completely unprofessional.

Todd turned to Barnaby, shutting the voice in his head out. "I'll be back in a few days, if your sitter says it's all right, and we'll see about getting you out of that cage to stretch your wings. *If* you can behave yourself."

"Nincompoop," Barnaby said agreeably.

He turned and saw Alice's smiling face, and all of his stern thoughts fell away.

Dang it, Alice...what are you doing to me?

6

ANNA

"Chicken cacciatore," Beckett announced, setting the casserole dish on the table with a flair.

"Yuck," said Teddy.

"You love chicken," Beckett reminded his grandson with a chuckle.

"Yuck, yuck, yuck," the toddler repeated, eying the lumpy red sauce with suspicion as Beckett cut up a piece of chicken breast.

"It's just chicken and ketchup," Anna encouraged the little boy.

"Cattup?" Teddy asked, clearly intrigued now.

His grandfather set a plastic plate down in front of him, innocuous squares of chicken next to a pool of red sauce. Teddy lowered his face to the plate and dipped the very tip of his tongue into the sauce.

"Cattup!" he agreed happily and began to eat.

Beckett served Anna and then himself each a heaping plate of polenta, chicken, and vegetables. The polenta was rich and creamy, the perfect accompaniment to the tangy cacciatore, but Anna pushed her food around on her plate.

She wasn't hungry.

"Don't tell me *you* don't like chicken and ketchup, now," Beckett teased.

"I *lub* kitten cattup," Teddy said. "Nana, wook! *Big* boy bite!" He shoved the biggest piece of chicken into his mouth, and Beckett watched like a hawk until it was safely swallowed.

Anna grinned at the little boy. She cut off a big bite of her own, and put it into her mouth with exaggerated motions. "Mmm!" she said, still chewing. "Goood!"

Teddy giggled and turned his attention to his food.

"Nana a big boy, too!"

"It really is delicious," Anna told Beckett after she'd chased the chicken down with a swig of wine. "I just don't have much of an appetite."

"Are you—" Beckett began, interrupted by an "Oh-ohh" as a pool of milk spread across the table.

"I've got it," Anna said. She jumped up to grab a roll of paper towels, covering the puddle just as Teddy tried to splash in it.

"My fault," Beckett said with an abashed grin. "I keep losing his sippy cups."

"There are two in my car," Anna said. "I'll grab them so he has one for bedtime."

By the time Anna had washed the sippy cups and filled one with warm milk, Beckett had given Teddy a quick bath and was in the process of wrestling him into a bedtime onesie.

"Nana!" Beckett crowed happily when Anna appeared in the doorway. "Nanna, weed books!"

"I would love to read you a bedtime story," Anna told him. Teddy ran over to hug her legs, and Anna felt such a surge of love for the little boy that tears sprang to her eyes. She had chosen a globe-trotting career over motherhood; she had certainly never expected to become a grandmother.

How did she get so lucky?

Beckett kissed her on the cheek on his way out.

"I'll handle the clean-up," he said.

Anna tucked Teddy into the big-boy bed that he had recently graduated to. The handsome wooden crib he had used at their house prior was a sturdy antique, so Anna and Beckett had given it to her nephew Gabe and his wife Sasha for Grace. Anna was excited to meet her newest little niece; she wondered if she would have the chance to get to know Beth before baby Grace made her arrival. Would Beth and Nikki really stay in Bluebird Bay long enough to join them for Thanksgiving?

"Nana, books!" Teddy insisted.

"Books!" Anna agreed, grabbing a pile from his shelf. Toddlers were so good at pulling adults back into the present moment. When did people lose that ability to be so completely present?

Teddy rejected a few of his wordier board books before they finally settled into *Goodnight Moon*. Anna's mother, Rose, had read it to her three girls so often that Anna could recite the book without even looking at the words. She finished, and Teddy tapped his fingertips together, a sign she'd come to learn meant *"more"*. By the fourth reading, he was sound asleep.

Anna set the book down and looked at his angelic little face. She reached to brush a tuft of hair away from his eyes.

"Another tale of the Dread Pirate Roberts?" She heard Pop's voice as clearly as if he were sitting right next to her.

Mom had mostly been the one to read to them. Pop had never had much patience for books. But sometimes, when Mom was too tired to read, Pop would tell them stories. He made them up on the fly, it seemed. Sometimes they would be a retelling of a classic tale. Other times he would take the snatches of books that he heard as Rose read to the girls, and co-opt some character for a tale of his own. The Dread Pirate Roberts had been their favorite for years. It got so that it all blended together in Anna's mind, and she could never quite remember what had happened in the books Mom read versus what Pop invented on the nights that he filled in. Sometimes he told true stories — more or less — about his youth, a run-in with a black bear, the summers he spent on fishing boats, the one that got away... Anna could even remember a bawdy limerick or two.

She wondered if Eric — Nikki's father, and technically Anna's, as well — would have done as much. He had met Anna's mother at the library, so he must've liked books. Had he read to his daughters and son, or told them stories?

For a moment, she felt tempted to ask Nikki, but Anna shoved the thought away. It felt disloyal to Pop. There was enough family drama to deal with here in Bluebird Bay without adding her absentee father to the mix.

Anna kissed Teddy on the crown of his head, turned on his nightlight, and gently closed the door to his room. Downstairs, the dining table was spotless. The dinner dishes sat in the drying rack, and Beckett was closing the oven.

"I thought I might tempt you with dessert," he said. "I put in some brownies."

Anna crossed the kitchen and kissed him.

"You're amazing," she told him with complete sincerity.

Beckett's hands were steady on her shoulders.

"What's on your mind, babe?"

"You know me too well," she sighed.

"That's a good thing." Beckett's tone was firm, but there was a question in his eyes.

Anna stood on tiptoe to kiss him again.

"It's the best thing," she told him. "You and Teddy both."

"Agree," Beckett said, pulling her close. "I didn't get to do the cozy family life thing the first time around. I was working nights when Austin was small, and things between his mom and I were never... Anyway, I love it when you and Teddy and I are together. I don't think I've ever felt so content in all my life." He kissed her neck and pulled away. "Don't think that I haven't noticed that you avoided my question."

Anna grinned and grabbed the bottle of wine they had opened for dinner.

"That kind of conversation, is it?" Beckett raised his eyebrows and lifted two glasses off of the drying rack.

"Aren't they all, lately?" Anna headed for the couch. She sank into the worn leather with a sigh as he joined her and poured two glasses of wine. "It's nothing new, really. I just... I feel like the hits just kept coming, you know? First, Paul died and Steph was inconsolable, and then everything with my health...it brought back all of this stuff I never really dealt with when Mom died. Then Pop, the dementia and the fire and losing him. Our Hawaii trip was like a reset, you know? I felt like I could finally catch my breath again — and bam!

Nikki shows up, and I have a whole family living two hours away."

Anna paused and took a deep drink.

"You forgot the part where you faced down a madman with a gun," Beckett added with a rueful half-smile.

"Twice!" Anna's laugh sounded slightly unhinged to her own ears, and she took a deep breath.

"Beth coming to town isn't a bad thing. I'm actually excited to get to know her. It's just... I feel like my nervous system can't even handle *little* shocks right now. Does that make sense?"

"It makes complete sense," Beckett replied.

"I used to be unshakable," said Anna with a shrug. "Lately, I feel really...tired."

"You are a rock star," he said in a grave voice, and leaned forward to kiss her. Settling back into the couch, he continued, "What you've been through would fry *anyone's* nerves. I'm amazed that you've held up as well as you have."

She took a deep breath.

"I guess that's partly why I'm worried about Beth. We invited them to Thanksgiving at Steph's house, but... God, I can't imagine walking into a family holiday dinner at Lena's as an *adult*, much less walking into a foreign Thanksgiving as a nineteen-year-old kid."

"They're adaptable at that age," Beckett said. "Austin used to bring roommates and girlfriends home for Thanksgiving when he was in college. It's no big deal to them."

"Maybe. I just hope that she doesn't feel... *other*. The way I felt when I found out about Eric. Like I didn't know where I fit anymore. I hope Nikki allowing her to choose to stay here was the right call."

"Letting people make their own decisions is almost always the right call." Beckett squeezed Anna's shoulder. "So is leaving the door open to family."

Anna still had her doubts. She imagined how hard it would be for her to drop into a family holiday in Cherry Blossom Point, to watch the siblings she had never met interact with each other and with her biological father, all the while painfully aware that she didn't quite belong there.

"All I can do is go with the flow and make sure I do my best to make her feel welcome," she said finally.

The older she got, the more she was getting like Cee-cee, wanting to fix everything for everyone.

A timer went off in the kitchen, and Beckett went to turn off the oven. He returned with two bowls filled with hot, fudgy brownies and vanilla-bean ice cream.

"Dinner of queens," he said with mock seriousness as he handed Anna her bowl.

She laughed, feeling a stab of guilt.

"I really did like the chicken cacciatore," she told him. "I bet it will be even better tomorrow."

"Sure," Beckett said in mock annoyance. "Spent my whole day hunched over a hot stove..."

"These brownies are reeeally good," Anna purred, savoring the warm, gooey chocolate.

He shrugged and grinned. "They're from a box. But yeah, it's the good stuff. And I added chocolate chips."

"Perfect," Anna said, and they finished their dessert in comfortable silence.

She headed into the kitchen to wash their bowls, and as

she finished the dishes, Beckett appeared behind her and began to rub her shoulders. All the thoughts weighing her down faded away on a long, contented sigh under his strong hands.

"Come to the couch," he murmured in her ear, "and I'll rub your feet."

"You don't have to tell me twice," Anna said, letting him lead her back into the living room. Beckett pulled her stockinged feet up into his lap and ran his thumbs firmly along her arches. Anna's eyes closed, and she sank into the couch.

"You're going to spoil me," she said.

"Not possible," Beckett replied. "You worry so much about everyone else. You do so much for me, and for Teddy. I like it when you let me take care of you once in a while."

His hands worked their way up her calves.

"Okay," she agreed groggily.

"Everything will work out for the best," he assured her. "It always does."

When Anna's phone buzzed twenty minutes later, she lifted her face from a drool spot on the throw pillow.

"I should've turned it off," Beckett said with a grin. "You were snoring like a lumberjack, and it was the cutest thing."

"Oh, sure. Real cute," she said as she sat up and reached for her phone. Blinking the sleep from her eyes, she peered down at the screen to see a text from Cee-cee.

What are you doing Friday, daytime?

Anna mentally ran through her schedule before texting back cautiously.

Besides work in the morning until 11 am, nothing. Why?

Cee-cee's reply pinged back right away.

I need a partner in crime for a little light espionage. You in?

Anna shook her head with a groan. She should probably ask some questions, like "Why?", "Where?", or "What's going on?".

But, really, there was no point. Cee-cee was her sister, and there was only one answer to the question.

She typed back quickly and hit send.

I'm your Huckleberry.

7

TODD

ANOTHER EAR-SPLITTING YOWL ECHOED from the far
corner of the room, and Todd winced. First thing that
morning, he had extracted a cracked and rotten tooth from
the mouth of an elderly cat named Winston, who was now
awake and feeling salty.

"When did Mrs. Herrick say she was coming in?" Todd
asked the receptionist.

"An hour ago," Nadine replied. "I'll double-check that
she's en route before I leave for lunch. Can I get you
anything?"

"No," Todd said. "Thank you. I'll run around the corner
for a sandwich. I just want to take another look at Chuck's
iguana. I don't know what that thing has been eating, but we
might need to make time for a coeliotomy this afternoon."

Nadine nodded. "You decide by the time I'm back from
lunch, and if we need to, I can reschedule our last few
appointments. There's nothing urgent the rest of the day, just
new client visits."

He'd have preferred seeing the new puppies and kittens over poking around in iguana guts, but such was life.

"Thank you."

The woman was a godsend. Todd had created an automated booking system in hopes that he could manage the calls and wouldn't have to hire a new receptionist, but it was all just too much. Nadine had only been working with him for two weeks, and already the place was transformed. She had been slowly finishing the work job he'd started, automating all the client charts, and handled the front room with a grandmotherly care that kept both pets and their owners calm until it was their turn to see him.

He was just putting Iggy back in his tank when the door to the exam room opened. He looked up, surprised that Nadine would be back from lunch so soon, but found the original Dr. Ketterman standing there.

Todd smiled.

"Hey, Mom. What brings you in?"

"I was in the area and wanted to pop by to say hello," Stephanie said brightly.

Checking up on him, then. He had tried to mask his exhaustion the past few times he'd seen her, but Stephanie Ketterman was no fool.

"Always good to see you." He pulled her close and dropped a kiss on the top of her head. "And, hey, since you're here..."

He crossed the room and opened Iggy's file. The radiograph that he had taken that morning looked normal, as far as he could tell. And he hadn't seen anything on the ultrasound, either. But there was clearly something wrong with the iguana... his owner said that he had hardly eaten in days, and there seemed to be sore spots on his abdomen. He handed the radiograph to his mother.

"Anything jumping out at you?" he asked.

Stephanie frowned at the picture and crossed the room to examine it in front of a light. "There does seem to be some kind of obstruction..." she murmured.

"Where?" Todd demanded. He went to look over her shoulder.

"See that foamy bit, just there?" Stephanie pointed.

"That looks like normal food and gas."

Steph shook her head. "I don't think so. I think there is something there. It's not like a big, solid mass, that's why it's hard to see. He might have eaten a bit of cloth, or some cotton balls... iguanas eat the strangest things sometimes."

Todd slumped onto a stool. "If I reschedule the new patient visits in favor of a coeliotomy, do you think they'll jump ship and go to that vet in Rockport instead?"

Stephanie wasn't listening, though. She had that faraway, super-focused look on her face as she palpated the iguana's belly.

"There's definitely a buildup of gas. Something is going on for sure."

"So coeliotomy it is," he said with a sigh. "I've just got to figure out where to move the other appointments." He was packed to the gills, and the thought of cutting even deeper into his limited hours off made him wince.

His mother stepped away from the tank and turned to him with a smile. "And no, I don't think the new clients will jump ship. But I'll tell you what. You handle the surgery, and I'll take the check-ups. Ask Nadine to have them come in tomorrow afternoon."

He nodded and shot her a grateful smile. "Only if you're sure. I can juggle it, no problem, if—"

"I wouldn't have offered if I couldn't do it, so stop," she shot back with a shake of her head. "You are turning into a workaholic, and it's not healthy. I'm glad you brought Nadine on, but that doesn't mean adding more to your plate to fill the time you've saved by hiring her. Got it?"

She had that fiery light in her eyes and he knew better than to argue. "Got it, Sarge."

Her lips quirked into a half-smile. "Now, for the important stuff. I brought coffee. And a sandwich for you, too."

"Thanks, I haven't eaten yet."

"I figured," Stephanie replied.

His mother, the mind reader. If he wasn't so hungry and relieved, he might be worried at just how well she knew him.

She led him to his office, where she had set his lunch out on his desk.

"Where's yours?" Todd asked.

"It's almost two, you know," Stephanie admonished. "I taught my first class at seven, and I ate before noon. I wanted to eat early because I'm picking up food later to have dinner with Jeff and Cee-cee, and I wanted to be good and hungry."

Todd sat down and took a grateful sip of coffee.

"Usually I grab a granola bar or something because we've been taking our lunches later in the day," he told her. "Sometimes people can only manage to bring their pets in on their lunch break, so—"

"I'm worried about you, Todd." Stephanie sat down across from him. "I'm so proud, but I'm worried. Your plans to pile on the new patients were made before I decided to fully retire. You can't keep going like this alone."

"There's just a flood of new patients right now," Todd said through a mouthful of bacon-lettuce-tomato. He swallowed and continued, "We've been a little swamped just getting them up to date on shots and all, but that will slow down. It's not too many patients to carry long-term. It's just been a bit much all at once."

"You need to find more balance," Stephanie pressed. "You worked so hard all through college. You don't have to build the business up so fast so quickly. We're not hurting for money. Take it slower. Cut back to normal hours."

The clinic had been on a downslide when Todd had first taken over, but he didn't want to remind his mother of that. It hadn't been her fault. Between losing the love of her life and caring for Pop and nursing Aunt Anna through her cancer treatments, his mom had been through so much. She had built this practice from the ground up, and he would make sure it continued on, bigger and stronger than ever.

"This sandwich is really good," he said.

"Make time to eat, Todd. Please. Earlier in the day."

"So you're meeting Jeff for dinner?" Todd parried, deftly changing the subject. "How is he doing with Mick and all?" Guilt prickled at him as he realized he'd only seen his brother a couple times in the past weeks.

Steph narrowed her eyes slightly at this bit of evasiveness, but she let it slide.

"I don't think I've ever seen Jeff so happy," Stephanie said. "Not since he was a little kid."

"Not everyone's cut out for college."

"No," his mom agreed slowly. "It's not for everyone. Jeff

was such an active, physical kid. And he always loved building things. Remember the LEGO years? I always thought that might translate into, I don't know, architecture or something." She met Todd's eyes. "All I want is for you all to be happy."

"Me, and Jeff, and Sarah, and your sisters, and yoga students, and the pets that come through here, and their owners, and Ethan, and on and on..." Todd chuckled. "It's a big ask. No one's happy all the time."

"Okay, I admit it," Stephanie said in a light tone. "I want the people I love to be mostly happy *most* of the time. Insanity!" She chuckled.

The bell on the reception area door jangled and Todd popped the last of his sandwich into his mouth with a frown.

"My next patient must be early."

He and his mother stood and made their way into the waiting room.

"Hi there, welcome to—"

He broke off as he locked eyes with a flustered-looking Alice.

"I'm sorry to just pop in...are — are you open?"

She stood just inside the front door, clutching a box to her chest. For a brief and morbid moment, Todd wondered if it contained Barnaby. But no, it was too small. He had a brief flashback of playing twenty questions on family road trips and heard Jeff's eight-year-old voice in his brain.

Is it smaller than a breadbox?

Todd made his way over to Alice, and his heart sped. Her cheeks were pink from the brisk winds, her black curls were bouncy and completely free of dust and grime, and the floral-patterned dress over a pair of black leggings she'd chosen looked freshly laundered. She smiled uncertainly, and Todd realized that he was staring.

Again.

He cleared his throat.

"We're open," he assured her. "Just took a late lunch break. Is everything okay?"

"Oh, yes. I'm fine. And Barnaby's fine. I mean, he's not *fine*...he's still kind of a jerk to me, but not any worse. No more feather plucking, far as I can tell. He's been eating lots of fresh food, and he's just about destroyed that toy you bought him."

Todd grinned. "That's what it's there for."

Alice's eyes flicked between him and Stephanie, who came to stand beside him.

"Sorry," Todd said quickly. "It's been a long day. Alice, this is my mom, Stephanie. Stephanie, this is Alice."

Alice grinned, and it was like looking into the sun.

"The original Dr. Ketterman!" she said, reaching out to shake Steph's hand. "Pleased to meet you."

"Likewise," Stephanie said with a wide smile.

"I sort of inherited a great green macaw," Alice told her. "Temporarily. Hopefully. My great-aunt broke her hip and I'm taking care of Barnaby while she recuperates. Todd's been helping because the bird hates me." She thrust out the box that she held, and Todd accepted it.

"I made banana bread," she said, tucking her hands into the pockets of her dress. "As a thank you. For the apples and bird toys and everything."

"That's so lovely of you. Banana bread is one of Todd's favorites," his mother said, beaming. She shot a glance at Todd before making a big show of looking at her watch.

"Would you look at the time? I really should get going," she said with a flutter of her hand. "I'm going to the shop to help Cee-cee do some cupcake decorating before we pick up dinner for the boys later. It was *lovely* to meet you, Alice."

Stephanie gave Todd a significant look as she walked away, complete with raised eyebrows and a knowing smile. It would have been embarrassing if Alice had been looking at her, but she wasn't.

Her eyes were firmly on Todd.

"Say hi to Aunt Cee-cee for me," Todd called after his mother as she hurried to the door. "And thanks for lunch, Mom."

Steph blew him a kiss and let the door swing shut behind her. Todd realized he was still holding the banana bread in front of him like it was a bomb, so he turned and set it on the counter before tucking his hands into his pockets.

"You didn't have to do that," he said. A tiny line appeared between Alice's eyebrows, and he rushed on, "But thank you. Really, it was so thoughtful."

Come on, Todd, be cool. Or at least, I don't know, normal?

"You clean up nice," he found himself murmuring as he stared at her.

So much for cool.

He resisted the urge to smack himself on the head, but Alice was grinning.

"It's a wonder what not being covered in decades-old grime can do for a girl," she shot back with a wink. "Plus, band nerds know a thing or two about how to present a pleasing picture. But I'll tell you one thing — I'm never wearing another black dress. All those years playing in orchestras... ugh. It was either a navy blue uniform or a black dress. When they put me in my coffin, it had better be in a yellow sundress. And sandals."

"Packing light for the afterlife?"

"Take me to the land of eternal summer," she agreed with an airy wave.

Todd laughed, marveling at how a sentence or two from this woman could erase the heavy stress that he had been carrying around all day.

"I can smell that bread from here, and I can't resist any longer." He reached for the box of banana bread and broke off a piece. It was still warm as he went to pop a bite into his mouth. Before he got there, though, Alice jumped forward, grabbing his hand. A wave of heat went through his body, as he blinked at her in surprise.

"Sorry!" she said nervously. "I forgot to ask if you have any allergies. Walnuts."

Todd grinned down at her. "Not a one."

"Oh good." Alice let her hand drop and he felt a surprising stab of loss. He resisted the urge to grab her hand again, and ate the bite of bread instead.

"So frigging good," he muttered around the moist bit of cake. He wasn't exaggerating. Sweet from the chocolate chips, with the nuts giving all that pillowy softness some texture. He would be surprised if his Aunt Cee-cee could make it better.

Alice beamed. "I'm glad you like it."

Todd took another bite, which he immediately regretted as they stood there in awkward silence. He swallowed and asked, "So Barnaby's doing better, then?"

Alice's smile faded and she shrugged. "I guess. He's screaming less, and seems to be less agitated. I've got to admit, though, we still haven't bonded. I care about the old guy because I know how much Auntie Louise loves him, but he's a lot. The house is a lot." She leaned on the counter and sighed. "Honestly, it's all kind of a lot at once, and I'm going a little crazy, cleaning all day with no one but Barnaby to talk to."

She pulled off a piece of banana bread and ate it. This seemed to cheer her.

"Huh, you were right! This did turn out good!" She took another bite and smiled. "Honestly, baking the bread was the perfect excuse to get out of that place for a few hours. I downloaded a couple episodes of *The Price is Right* and left my laptop running for Barnaby. That seemed to cheer him up a bit."

Todd chuckled and searched for a topic that would keep Alice there a few minutes longer.

"Have you found anything interesting under the stacks of newspapers?"

"I haven't even *started* on the newspapers," Alice groaned. Then, she brightened. "I did find some things in Auntie's closet, though."

"Yeah?" Todd said through a mouthful of banana bread.

"I found some stock papers. Some are so old that they were written out by hand. I don't know if they're worth anything, but they're pretty cool."

"That's fascinating," Todd said. "Maybe there's a gold mine under all that junk. Do you need a mining partner?"

What did you just say? the critical voice in Todd's head muttered. *What IS it with you today?*

"I wouldn't turn down the help," Alice said with a wide smile. "But I warn you, it's mostly just 80s magazines and parrot poop. Only every so often does something neat pop up."

"Consider me forewarned," he replied easily. He knew he should take the out. With a month's worth of his own household chores piling up, he really shouldn't be committing his free time. But as he looked down into Alice's warm, open face, he realized the chores could wait.

God, she was pretty...

They both startled a little as the phone rang.

"One sec," he told Alice as he reached over the counter to pick it up.

"Hey, Dr. Ketterman?" a woman asked.

"Speaking."

"This is Lizzy? I brought in my yellow lab, Daisy?" Every sentence the woman uttered was lilted up at the end like a question. "You said she was pregnant? Well, she didn't eat her food today, and Daisy *never* says no to food. She's just been lying around all day. I'm getting really worried."

Todd grabbed the pen-and-paper appointment book that Nadine insisted on using alongside their computer system. He looked at the packed schedule and sighed. So much for getting to the gym before work tomorrow morning...

"How's eight o'clock tomorrow sound?" he asked.

"Great. Thank you so much, Dr. Ketterman! See you then."

"See you at eight."

He hung up and penciled in the appointment before turning his attention back to Alice.

"Sorry," he began, and Alice cut in.

"That's okay," she said, toying with the hem of her dress.

"You're busy, and you didn't sign up to be on an episode of *Hoarders*. I mean, neither did I, not *knowingly,* but—"

"I'd like to," Todd said.

Alice looked up at him, dark eyes wide.

"I'd like to help," he added. "And if I can't make time for a treasure hunt with a friend, then what am I even doing? Plus, I know we can make more progress with Barnaby the more time I spend with him. I need him to trust me enough to give him a proper exam and make sure there's no physical issues adding to his stress."

"Okay, if you're sure..." Alice agreed hesitantly. "When's good? Do you have a day off?"

"Saturday? I still have a few appointments in the morning," he admitted sheepishly, "but I'm free after ten."

"You might be getting more than you bargained for." Alice seemed to be trying for a light tone, but there was some real hesitation there, too. "I didn't want to lead with this, but I swear I smelled a dead body. I haven't even opened the hall closet yet. I'm ninety-nine percent certain there's a decomposed person in there."

"Or Barnaby the first," Todd said gravely, and Alice laughed.

There was a long pause. One that made him want to lean in and—

The front door slammed open and Mrs. Herrick rushed in like a hurricane.

"Where's Winston?" she exclaimed. "I'm so sorry, I got held up at work. Where is he? Is his little toothy woothy okay?"

A yowl sounded from the back room, and Mrs. Herrick

rushed through the metal door marked with a sign that said *Staff and Patients Only*.

When Todd turned around, Alice was walking towards the exit. She glanced back and gave him a little wave over her shoulder.

"I'll see you Saturday," she said with a chuckle.

"Saturday," Todd echoed.

Dead body or not, Todd thought as she walked out the door, all he truly wanted was an afternoon with Alice.

8

NIKKI

Nikki stood at the window of their one-bedroom apartment, admiring the sliver of ocean that she could see between buildings.

"It's sunny out," she said over her shoulder, "and it doesn't look too windy today. Do you want to take a walk on the beach?"

"Not really," Beth said. She looked from her phone to the television and back again.

Nikki frowned at her daughter and turned back to the window. Beth had hardly met Nikki's gaze since she'd blown into town. Nikki had thought that they'd gotten off to a good start with Monster Mac and *Gilmore Girls*, but Beth had been binge watching the series for the past day and a half, from the time she got up, to the time Nikki went to bed at night. This morning, she'd grabbed a bowl of breakfast cereal and headed right back to the couch that she had slept on. She was willing to let Nikki feed her, or sit and watch the show with her, but any attempt to pull her out of her Netflix-induced coma had been stonewalled.

Nikki had suggested meeting up with Anna more than once, but despite Beth's insistence that they stay in town so she could get to know her aunt, she had found one reason or another to beg off. She was falling deeper and deeper into this funk, and something needed to change.

The credits began to roll on the latest episode, and Nikki grabbed the TV remote from the coffee table. She turned it off, and Beth looked at her like a bear that had been woken from its hibernation.

"Let's get some fresh air," Nikki said.

Beth's eyes narrowed. "Sure. Open a window."

The thin veneer of Nikki's patience cracked. "What's the point of paying for this place if you're just going to sit and watch TV every day?" she demanded. "You can do that at home."

For a split second, the sullen teenager fell away and Nikki glimpsed her little girl, hurt and frightened. Her ire melted, and she sat down on the corner of the couch.

"Come on, Beth. At least let me show you around Bluebird Bay. We can get a bite to eat, maybe buy some more groceries?"

"Fine." Beth shoved the blankets from her legs and trudged off to the bathroom.

Nikki quickly pulled on some jeans and a sweater, and then sat waiting for Beth to get ready. When her daughter finally reappeared, Nikki suggested Mo's Diner.

"Sure," Beth said.

The monosyllabic replies continued on the ride to the restaurant. Nikki asked Beth about her classes, her roommate, her friends... but nothing she said worked to entice Beth out of her sullen silence. When they pulled up to the diner, Beth was out of the car almost before it came to a full stop. She was in the door by the time Nikki locked the car and followed.

Nikki walked in, and Eva came out from behind the counter to give her a hug.

"Hey there, stranger!" Eva said cheerfully as she squeezed Nikki. "Long time no see!"

She looked from Beth to Nikki and back again.

"You must be the prodigal daughter!" Eva said. She pulled Beth in for a hug but the girl's arms hung at her sides as she stared at Nikki with wide eyes.

"I am so happy to meet you," Eva said as she released her. "Your mother thinks you hung the moon, do you know that? She has nothing but good things to say about you."

Beth blushed, and Nikki glimpsed a hint of a smile.

"This is Eva," Nikki told her daughter. "She hired me at the diner when I came to Bluebird Bay."

"Your mother has been a godsend," Eva declared. "She's just a whirlwind of energy and fresh ideas. Me? I don't have a creative bone in my body. Beth, your mom tells me you're doing really well in school. She misses you like crazy, I can tell, but I think her stay in Bluebird Bay has done her some good. We'll be sorry to see her go, I'll tell you that much. I don't know where I'll find another cook with your mother's work ethic, or her way with a recipe."

An impatient customer was waving, and Eva flashed Nikki a smile. "You girls sit down. I'll be right over."

"Do you want to sit there by the window?" Nikki asked her daughter.

"So was this part of your master plan?" Beth muttered, her tone acidic.

Nikki froze and stared at her, nonplussed. "I'm not sure what you mean..."

"You thought that if you dragged me around town and showed me how much everybody here loves you, I would forgive you for starting a whole new life without me?"

"I haven't started a new life, Beth," Nikki said in a low voice, hurt to the core at the accusation. "I just wanted to get you out of the apartment and let you meet some of the people I've come to care about..."

"I'm glad you have all these new people to care about," Beth said in an angry voice. She pulled the front door open with a clang and rushed out. Nikki followed her, but Beth was speed walking down the sidewalk.

"Where are you going?" Nikki shouted after her.

"For a walk," Beth shouted over her shoulder. "You wanted me off the couch. I'm off the couch!" A moment later, she disappeared around the corner.

Nikki stood there for a long moment before heading back inside Mo's and slumping into the booth.

For the past nineteen years, she and Beth had been more than mother and daughter. Beth had been her world. The light of her life. Where had she gone wrong? If she had stayed put in Cherry Blossom Point, maybe things would've been all right—

She shut that thought down instantly. Steve would have gone there instead, and other members of her family could've gotten hurt. But if she hadn't been seeing Mateo, would Steve still be alive? Maybe that was the question Beth was grappling with. While her daughter had sworn Steve's death wasn't the cause of her pain, it was possible that this was all too fresh for her to even really pinpoint what was wrong.

While Nikki couldn't find it in her to regret Steve's death —being safe from him permanently was like a giant weight off her back—there were still repercussions.

"Crap," Nikki muttered under her breath.

"Yeah," Eva replied as she slid in across from her. "Sometimes life is crap," the older woman agreed with a sage nod. "You look like you just got hit by a truck, kiddo. You want some blueberry pie?"

"No," Nikki said. "Thank you. I'm not hungry."

"You don't need to be hungry to enjoy a slice of pie," Eva replied. When Nikki didn't return her smile, Eva reached out and took her hand.

"I just want to make things right with Beth," Nikki said. "But I don't know how."

"Give her some time," Eva said, squeezing her hand sympathetically. "She'll come around. She's punishing you for making a new life for yourself. The tricky thing is, she doesn't even know that she's doing it. Lord, when I think of the worry that I put my mother through... of course, it all felt perfectly justified at the time."

Nikki took a few deep breaths and managed a tiny smile for her friend.

"I shudder to think of the decisions that I was making at that age," Nikki agreed. "I want her to know I'm here for her. We were always so close. I never thought it would be like this. If she goes back to school with this wedge between us and she has no one to talk to about the way she's feeling, what if she turns to some idiot boy for comfort?"

Or worse, a full-grown narcissist. Please, God, don't let her repeat my mistakes.

"And there is already all that pressure with the drinking

and the drugs...If she bottles all this up, is she going to seek solace that way?"

Nausea rolled through her at the thought.

"She's a strong kid, just like her mom, so I don't think that's gonna happen. You're a smart cookie, and you love her. The answer will come to you before she heads back to school. And if not? Get her set up with some counseling out there." Eva gave Nikki's hand one last squeeze as she stood. "Now you hang out for a minute while I go box you up a couple slices of blueberry pie to go."

Eva was gone before Nikki could tell her that Beth didn't like blueberries...but she knew someone else who did.

She pulled her phone out of her purse and texted Mateo.

Are you home?

His answer came back immediately.

Yup.

Eva bustled back in with a white to-go bag and handed it to her as Nikki stood.

"On the house. It's your recipe, after all," Eva said with a rusty chuckle.

"Thank you," Nikki called as Eva strode off to greet a party of four that had just walked in. Nikki watched her bustle away, tired just looking at her. Where that woman got her energy at her age, Nikki had no idea. Maybe there was something to be said for a steady diet of blueberry pie and arguments with cantankerous old men.

Nikki's phone buzzed as she made her way to the door, and she winced as she looked down.

It was from her brother Jack, almost as if the very thought of cantankerous old men had somehow summoned him.

Gayle said Beth texted her and the two of you are staying

in Bluebird Bay for Thanksgiving??? What the hell is that about? These people are not your family, Nikki. Call me ASAP.

Double crap. She'd wanted another day or two with Beth alone to be sure that was what her daughter wanted to do before telling her siblings about the holiday. There was no point in getting them all riled up for nothing if things got even more strained here in Bluebird Bay. But Beth had taken matters into her own hand. Maybe it was her attempt to take control of something when everything else around her felt like chaos.

No matter the reason, it was done, and Nikki needed to figure out how to manage that mess.

A second message came hot on the heels of the first, this one also from Jack, but she pocketed her phone without reading it.

Jack hated waiting, and would get even hotter under the collar than he already was if she didn't get back to him, but too bad. She only had the energy for one crisis at a time, and her daughter was her number one priority.

The sky began to fade to twilight as she drove to Mateo's place. She turned a corner, and the sky in front of her was streaked orange and pink and purple. As she passed her old bungalow, she purposely avoided looking at it. It had been the site of one of the worst nights of her life, and she looked forward to Mateo moving to his new house so she could avoid this street altogether.

Nikki parked in front of Mateo's place and paused to send a message to Beth.

Text when you're home safe. Please.

She walked up the path, and Mateo opened the door

before she could even knock. At the sight of his welcoming smile, all of the emotion she had been holding in for the past hour came pouring out. She fell into his arms with a groan and buried her face in his shoulder.

"Beth hates me," she choked out, the words muffled against the worn cotton of his t-shirt.

Mateo held her tight and rocked her from side to side gently as she breathed in his comforting scent.

"Aw, babe, I'm so sorry." He drew back and led her to the couch. "I'm going to make us some tea. Take some deep breaths, and then I'll sit down and listen. Sound good?"

"Tea would be wonderful," she said with feeling. "Thank you."

A few minutes later, Mateo returned with two mugs. He settled onto the couch and handed one to Nikki.

"Spill," he said.

She shook her head and took a soothing sip of her tea.

"Nothing to spill, really," she told him. "She won't even talk to me. She just wants to burrow into the couch and alternate between screens. She had all three going at once yesterday. Netflix on the flat screen, text messages on her phone, and a school assignment on her laptop all at the same time."

Mateo smiled at her. "So she has friends to text with and she's keeping up with her schoolwork. That's good, at least?"

"I guess," Nikki said with a sigh. "She's not totally shutting down...I'm glad of that. But she definitely isn't interested in talking to me right now." She set her mug on the coffee table, and tea sloshed over the rim.

Mateo shook his head dubiously. "She's just had the shock of her life. Once she assured herself you were safe and inserted her presence into this new picture, she retreated while her subconscious works to integrate everything that's happened."

She cocked her head and eyed him curiously.

"Point is, I don't think this has much to do with you, at all. When a kid has an absentee parent, there's always this painful, precious hope that someday they'll be better. The magic pill, the right treatment center... and suddenly they're sane and you have that second parent you always—"

He cut off and seemed to settle back into the present, looking Nikki in the eyes.

"My mom was a paranoid schizophrenic," he told her softly. "As long as I can remember, she was in and out of hospitals and psych wards. There were good times, in between. A lot of them. I can remember her singing and dancing around the living room, holding my hands... But she was gone more than she was home. And, after a while, even when she was home she was mostly gone, you know?"

He was silent for a moment, and Nikki's stomach filled with instinctive dread.

"She took her own life when I was fourteen," he muttered softly.

"Oh, Mateo." Nikki scooted closer and ran a soothing hand up and down his back.

"I hadn't seen her in over a year. I was almost glad, when my dad told us. She was so terrified when she was sick. She saw the most horrific things. She suffered for so long. I figured that if she was in heaven, at least she could watch us with clear eyes. But part of me felt so lost, and I couldn't figure out why it mattered so much. She was hardly ever around."

"She was your mother. That had to have been incredibly difficult."

"And Steve was Beth's father," Mateo told her. "Despite her not remembering him being around, there is a very real possibility that Beth is grieving the father who would never be able to make amends for the hell he put you through. There will be no chance for redemption. No magic pill that will make him better and give her the dad she so desperately longed for. That hope died with Steve that night."

She nodded slowly as Mateo's words hit home.

"I wonder if she blames me...or us?"

Nikki knew rationally that Steve's actions had caused his demise, but there was no question that Nikki, Anna, and Mateo had all played some role in what transpired that night. Did Beth believe they could've handled things differently?

Nikki leaned in and rested her cheek on Mateo's shoulder.

"This sucks. I feel totally helpless."

"Maybe I could talk to her?" Mateo suggested. "I know what it's like to have a parent who couldn't *be* a parent. And I know what it's like to lose a parent to suicide."

Nikki found herself nodding. She was afraid of how Beth might react to Mateo — Nikki had never brought a man home to meet her daughter — but his experience might truly be of help.

Don't get ahead of yourself, Nik.

"I'll talk to her," she told Mateo.

Assuming she could even get Beth to give her the time of day, of course...

9

CEE-CEE

"NEARLY READY?" Cee-cee asked her daughter.

"Just a few more," Max murmured as she scanned the shelves in front of her. She had gone to an estate sale the day before and come away with boxes and boxes of old books. There were leather-bound classics and novels with rich, cloth covers. Cee-cee had her eye on a vintage set of Jane Austen books — maybe that would be her Christmas gift to Stephanie.

"Are there any Stephen King books that Gabe *hasn't* read?" she wondered aloud. He had been obsessed with Stephen King in high school, but didn't have much time to read these days. He might still appreciate an old favorite, though, or a new release.

"Probably not," Max said, still distracted. "Sorry, Mom, I'm trying to hurry. I just want to get these shelved before I go. I'm almost done."

"I'm in no rush, Maxy."

Cee-cee's heart swelled as she watched her only daughter move through the bookshop that she had created. Seeing Max succeed at something she loved brought Cee-cee such a deep sense of contentment. Finally, Max finished and locked up. They gathered their coats and headed out.

"How are things going with you and Dad?" Max asked as they strolled down the street a few minutes later.

Cee-cee frowned.

"You know what I mean," Max pressed. "What's going on with him?"

"I'm not sure yet."

"What do you mean 'yet'?"

"Let me handle it, Maxy." She didn't want her daughter involved in the scheme she'd cooked up. It wouldn't help Max's relationship with her father... and it was almost certainly illegal.

"What aren't you telling me?"

Cee-cee let out a heavy sigh. "Can you drop it, please? I'll tell you when I know something. Pinky swear."

"Have you met me?" Max asked lightly. "Don't you know I never learned to 'drop it'?"

"Just trust me on this one, would you?"

"Fine," Max grumbled. "But I'm not waiting around forever."

"You won't have to," Cee-cee replied, silently praying, yet again, that Nate's issue wasn't medical. He'd sworn it wasn't, but he'd looked so wan and tired. She shoved the thought aside as they approached the bar. A brightly colored sign announced, *Thirsty Thursday Happy Hour 4 - 7.*

"Technically, it should be Happy Hours, no?" Max asked, exaggerating the S.

"Don't call in the grammar police," Cee-cee said with a

laugh. "We'd have to pay full price — it's already six. Come on, let's see if our dates are here yet."

The place was packed, but Mick had secured them a booth by the window.

"Have you been waiting long?" Max asked.

"Nope. I got here about fifteen minutes early. The waitress seemed a little harried," he told them, "so I went ahead and ordered us some appetizers because I'm not sure when she'd have a chance to get back to us."

Cee-cee slid into the booth beside her fiancé and kissed him on the cheek.

"Did you order the potato skins?" Max asked.

"Of course," Mick replied with a chuckle.

Max beamed. "Thanks. I'm going to go up to the bar for drinks. Can I get you anything?"

"I'll take another pint of lager, if you please."

"Mom?"

"A glass of red," Cee-cee told her daughter. "Surprise me."

"You've got it. Hey, I see Ian! Back in a few." Max slipped into the crowd.

Mick put an arm around Cee-cee's waist, and she leaned in.

"How was your day?" he asked. His voice rumbled pleasantly through his chest. It sounded like home.

"Busy," she told him. "It was a good day. We had that birthday party for the little girl with celiac disease. Her mother about cried when I told her I'd be able to accommodate them. We did four different flavors, all gluten free. I made a rainbow of buttercream frostings and the mom supplied the decorations. The kids had a blast."

"I'm glad." Mick hugged her closer and murmured, "You smell delicious."

Cee-cee laughed. "I smell like cupcakes."

"Orange and vanilla," he said in the same low voice. "It's intoxicating."

"Hush," she giggled. "Here come the kids."

Max and Ian slid into the booth, each carrying two drinks.

"Look who I found at the bar?" Max said with a grin.

"Hey, Cee-cee. Mick," he said with a nod. "I followed your lead and got the lager," Ian added cheerfully as he slid one of the pint glasses to Mick.

"I got you a glass of merlot," Max told her mother, but Cee-cee only had eyes for Max's drink.

"What is *that*?" Cee-cee asked, gesturing to the muddy orange beverage.

"A pumpkin flip," Max said happily. "Don't let the unattractive appearance fool you. It's delicious. Like a pumpkin spice latte, but with bourbon instead of coffee."

As she spoke, the appetizers began to arrive. Mick had ordered grilled shrimp, a charcuterie board, and — of course — Max's favorite loaded potato skins. Cee-cee helped herself to a slice of brie drizzled with blueberry honey as Max took a huge bite of cheesy potato.

"We haven't seen much of you lately," Cee-cee said to Ian. "How's work going?"

"Great." Ian set down his beer and grinned. "The three escape rooms I have running are almost fully booked, and I've been working on a fourth. Actually..." he turned to Mick, "I was hoping I could hire you for some custom woodwork. Everyone loves the hidden doors in my other rooms, but the space I have left doesn't have anything like that. It's two small bedrooms upstairs, and I want to connect them somehow. We already have doors hidden behind bookshelves, and panels on the wall... I was thinking that for these rooms, we could use a big mirror that swings forward to let people step through to the next room. It would need to be automatic, so that it opens when they find the right switch or button."

"Sounds easy enough," Mick said agreeably.

"And Jeff could help," Cee-cee suggested.

"You're reading my mind," he agreed, kissing her on her temple. "It will be a great learning experience for him."

"How's he doing, anyway?" Max asked.

"Jeff? He's a treasure. The kid's got talent, and he's happy to work long hours, learn new techniques...loads of energy. We've completed nearly all my backlogged work in almost half the time it would have taken me to do everything myself. Giving me plenty of time for an escape room," he added with a grin.

"I was thinking you could do some special carvings, too? Like, there could be intricately carved bed posts and the carvings would have clues."

"Now *that* sounds like a fun project."

They continued chatting, each sharing fun ideas for the new room as they made their way through their snacks. When there was one potato skin left on the tray, Ian absently nudged it onto Max's plate as he talked. Cee-cee couldn't help but smile. She was so grateful that Max had found someone who treated her with the love and respect that she deserved, even when they were both so busy with their businesses.

She wished that Gabe and Sasha could have joined them,

but with Sasha working all the way up until her due date, and Gabe taking on as many clients as possible before winter, they had no energy to go out at night.

Cee-cee checked her watch and saw that it wasn't quite seven. She should order them some appetizers to go... maybe a couple of slices of cheesecake, too. She glanced around, but their waitress was nowhere to be seen.

"I'm going to order some food for Gabe and Sasha before we go," Cee-cee told them. "Any last requests?"

"I'm good," Mick said with a smile.

"Me too," Ian added.

Max popped up from the table. "I'll come with you. I want to get another boozy pumpkin thing."

Cee-cee smiled at her daughter. Arm in arm, mother and daughter wound through the crowd.

"Hey, I think I know that guy," Max said, veering them slightly off to the right.

Two men in suits sat at a high-top table and looked up as they approached.

"Hi, Cameron."

The man was looking at her blankly, and Max pressed on.

"Max...We met at that cocktail party at Indigo? This is my mom, Cee-cee."

"Pleased to meet you," the man said in a tone that suggested he was not at all pleased. He didn't introduce them to the man who sat across from him.

"Mom, Cameron's a friend of Dad's," Max continued slowly.

"N — not exactly a friend," Cameron stammered, glancing between Max and his companion. "More of a work acquaintance. We don't — We're not working together now, though."

Max stared at him blankly, and the stranger watched them through narrowed eyes. Something about his icy expression gave Cee-cee the shivers. Instinctively, she nudged Max with her shoulder and tugged her away.

"Enjoy your evening, gentlemen," Cee-cee said with a forced smile as they retreated.

"Weird. He was so friendly when we met him with Dad. I wonder what that was about?" Max asked, clearly confused.

"Who knows," Cee-cee said lightly, trying not to let her concern show. "You probably interrupted a serious conversation. Hey, what should I order for Gabe and Sasha? He loves mozzarella sticks, but I don't think they would travel well..."

Cee-cee kept chattering as they made their way to the bar, but there was a weight in the pit of her stomach.

She'd made some major wrong turns in her life, but over the past couple years, she'd learned to trust her gut more and more.

And her gut was definitely telling her Nate was in trouble.

10

ANNA

As ANNA STEPPED into Cee-cee's Cupcakes, the place was booming with cheerful chatter as the staff worked to satisfy an early lunch rush. The tables were full and people were standing around waiting on their to-go orders. Lots of faces, but none of them were Cee-cee's. Pete was working the register while Wanda cleaned up the annex room, which looked like it had hosted a birthday party for a horde of gremlins this morning.

"Hi, Wanda," Anna greeted the older woman. "My sister in the kitchen or upstairs?"

Wanda looked up from the frosting-and-sprinkles Armageddon she was working to sweep up.

"Oh, Anna, hey! Yeah, Cee-cee is downstairs finishing up. We have a couple of big orders going out this afternoon, a baby shower and an anniversary party."

"Got it. Thanks!" Anna jogged lightly down the stairs to the basement kitchen, where Cee-cee had dozens of cupcakes lined up on long, steel tables.

"Sorry," Cee-cee said with a groan, barely glancing up

from the mini-cakes she was frosting. "Give me fifteen minutes and we can head out."

"Perfect," Anna replied pertly, plopping her butt into a spinning stool and taking a quick whirl before slowing to a stop. "Just enough time to test out one of these cupcakes for you while you tell me what the hell is happening." She scanned the neat rows, looking for a wonky one, but coming up empty. "What, no rejects?" she demanded with a scowl.

"There're always rejects, Anna." Cee-cee jerked a thumb to the countertop against the wall. "I forgot to put the chocolate chips into the batter on those. You can take that whole dozen home with you."

Anna kicked off, rolling her stool over to the counter. "Nice! I'll take eleven home, and eat one now."

She plucked a vanilla frosted cake from the tray and rolled back to sit across from her sister.

"I still need to add the white chocolate filling to these cupcakes for a baby shower," Cee-cee said, holding up a bowl of blue frosting. She passed Anna the piping bag that she had been using. "You finish icing these orange creamsicle cakes for the Williamsons' anniversary party."

"Roger that," Anna replied before taking a massive bite of the moist cake. She set down her treat and swiped the excess crumbs off on her jeans as she finished chewing. "But it's time to fill me in. Who are we going all Murder She Wrote on? I need details, stat."

Cee-cee paused in her work, sliding her readers higher up on her nose as she shot Anna a guilty look. "So...you remember that guy Nate works with, Sam Hansen? He used to host the company holiday parties."

"Yes, I remember him," Anna scoffed, already getting a

bad feeling. "How could I forget? You dragged me to one a few years back to act as your buffer. I wound up having to practically wrestle him on the dance floor after he had too much nog in his eggnog. What about him?" she demanded suspiciously.

Cee-cee studied the cupcake in front of her intently. "Well, he's sort of part of my plan."

"Which is?" Anna asked, wondering if she even wanted to know now.

"To sneak into Nate's office when he's not there, go through his stuff, and see if I can find out what the hell he's hiding."

Anna set her frosting bag down on the table and paused to take a second bite of her cupcake. The cake was delicious, sure, but she needed a hot second to digest what her oldest sister was saying, and if she didn't have something to keep her mouth busy, she was going to blurt something she might regret. Something like—

"Damn it, Cee-cee, what is wrong with you?" she managed around her mouthful of cake. "He left you for some bimbo you both knew, couldn't even be bothered to tell you to your face, and he tried to steal your frigging dog. You have an awesome new guy who looks like he should be on the cover of Sexy Carpenters Monthly, and you're happier than you've ever been. What part of 'good riddance' don't you understand?" she demanded.

Why couldn't she just toss him out for good, sink or swim?

Because that isn't Cee-cee, a little voice reminded her.

Her sister stared at her through narrowed eyes.

"Sorry," Anna grumbled as she went to work on the

orange cupcakes. "I just thought we were done with that guy."

"He's the father of my children, Anna," Cee-cee murmured. "I'll never be totally done with him, not really. Romantically, yes. Of course. I've been done with that for a long time. But he's hiding something, and I get the sense that it's something dangerous..."

She filled Anna in on the strange encounter the night before with Cameron and then continued. "Is he bribing the wrong kind of people for permits, or doing their dirty work? Is he having financial issues? Did he screw someone somehow? Whatever it is, I won't let him derail Max and Gabe when they're finally both happy and doing so well."

"But *spying* on him? Are you sure that's a good idea?"

Cee-cee let out a humorless laugh. "No. Not in the least. But I need to know what's going on and that's my best option right now."

"Do you, though?"

Cee-cee stopped working and fixed her sister with a steely stare. "Are you my Huckleberry or not, Anna?"

Anna let out another long-suffering sigh, but then she met Cee-cee's eyes and nodded. "Always."

"All right, then. Get to work so we can get our sleuth on."

"Aye, aye, Captain."

They finished the cupcakes and boxed them up, including a variety pack earmarked for Nate's office. That was supposed to be Cee-cee's excuse for showing up out of the blue. She was dropping off cupcakes as a thank you for dinner. Not a cover Anna was particularly fond of — it reeked of desperation, the act of a woman trying to win back her philandering husband

— but what could she do? Cee-cee was her big sister, and Anna would be there for her come hell, high water, or whatever harebrained scheme Cee-cee dreamed up.

And it was harebrained, for sure.

Forty minutes later, they were parked in front of the massive office building about to do something that was morally wrong, at best, and illegal, at worst.

On the flip side, it couldn't happen to a nicer guy.

Anna cracked her knuckles, and then her neck.

"All right, team. Ready?"

Cee-cee nodded, looking a little green around the gills.

"Yep. As ready as I'll ever be."

They exited the car and headed into the building.

As they approached the main desk, Cee-cee plastered a Stepford smile on her face and walked straight up to the receptionist.

"Good afternoon, Denise! We were passing by on our way to lunch," she told the woman brightly, "and I wanted to drop off some cupcakes for Nate. Is he in?"

"Hi, Cee-cee," the other woman said with a slightly baffled smile. "Um, actually, no, he's not in. He went to lunch a little while ago and I don't expect him back until at least 2 or so."

No surprise there, since Anna had called before they left the shop, pretending to be a prospective client, and had been given that same information.

"Aw, sorry I missed him," Cee-cee said with regretful *snick* of the tongue. "I'll just go put them in his office quick?" Cee-cee said it like a question, but she was already turning to go. She stopped short as Denise replied.

"Oh, don't trouble yourself. You can leave them with me and I'll give them to Nate when he gets back."

Anna winced. She'd been hoping it wouldn't come to this. In fact, she'd even made a deal with God that if it *didn't* come to this, she would give up coffee for Lent next year.

But no good deed went unpunished, it seemed.

"Oh, sure! Thanks so much." She made like she was about to hand over the box and then paused. "Hey, so long as we're here, could you tell me if Sam Hansen is in? We'd love to say hello."

"Sam is always in," the receptionist replied with a snort. "He eats lunch at his desk." She pressed a button and spoke into the intercom. "Sam, I have Cee-cee Burrows—erm, *Sullivan* here to see you."

Sam Hansen appeared almost cartoonishly fast, looking exactly as Anna remembered him. Expensive suit, smarmy smile, and about a pound of gel in his thinning hair. His smile broadened as he caught sight of Anna.

"Oh my, it's two of the Sullivan girls!" he boomed. "To what do I owe the pleasure?"

"We were on our way to lunch," Cee-cee told him, "and I wanted to bring some cupcakes by. Actually, I think there might be one with your name on it." She opened the box and pulled out one of her chocolate-raspberry concoctions. Anna's stomach rumbled. She had gotten so worked up about stupid Nate, she'd forgotten hers back at the shop. Maybe she could swipe one of these on their way out—

"This is amazing," Sam said, mouth half-full of chocolate ganache. "No one believed it when we heard you'd started your own business, you being the stay at home mom type, but wow. You've got talent."

The shock was evident in his tone and Anna had to resist the urge to pop him upside the head. What the hell was the "stay at home mom type", anyway? Pompous idiot.

But Cee-cee stayed admirably chill.

"Thank you so much," she cooed in a sickly-sweet tone that set Anna's nerves on edge. "Hey!" she said, brows shooting high as if she'd just come up with an amazing idea. "I know Anna would love a tour. Why don't you show her around while I go in and drop these on Nate's desk and leave him a quick note? I need to use the ladies' room, anyway."

"That sounds like a great idea," Sam purred. He had chocolate on his chin. Anna hated his stupid face.

"Yes," Anna agreed, trying not to roll her eyes as she attempted to match her sister's enthusiastic tone. "I've always loved looking at office buildings. They're so...corporate, you know?" she added with a smile. It felt stiff, but Sam didn't seem to notice as he hooked a clammy hand around her elbow and led her down the hallway.

"This place wasn't much to look at when I started here back in the day, but look at it now. How times have changed. We had a complete remodel back in 2010, and we've added even more since then. Just look at that paneling! That was my idea," he added in an exaggerated whisper close to her ear that brought a whiff of pepperoni on hot breath along with it. "And those paintings, those are the real deal. Beau coup bucks. I told Nate, I said, if we're going to bring in the big money clients, we have to look the part."

Anna shot Cee-cee a glare over her shoulder as Sam pulled her down the hallway.

Her sister owed her *big time*.

11

CEE-CEE

There was so much adrenaline pumping through Cee-cee's veins as she walked down the corridor that she felt like she'd gulped an entire pot of coffee, black. Her heart pounded with nerves, and she clutched the cupcake box so tight that it started to crumple.

This was crazy.

She could still back out... but the image of Anna's march-to-the-gallows face as Sam led her away propelled her onward. Anna might be the baby of the family, but Cee-cee had zero doubt that Anna could beat her up — and surely would if she found out that Cee-cee had handed her over to Sam for naught.

She reached the door to Nate's office and paused for a long moment to take a deep breath.

"You can do this," she murmured.

She glanced left, then right, before turning the knob. It gave way easily under her hand, as expected, and she let out a sigh of relief.

So far, so good.

She closed the door behind her and turned to face the room.

Now, where to start?

She looked around at the expanse of glossy wood and expensive carpet, and then headed for Nate's oversized desk. Setting down the box of cupcakes, she sidled around to the front and opened the nearest drawer. Business cards, loose change, rubber bands and pens.

Not exactly a smoking gun.

Cee-cee went to open the next drawer, only to find a pile of file folders that looked to be filled with nothing but real estate reports and permit applications. She was about to turn her attention to the bookshelf, but nearly jumped out of her skin when the office door swung wide. She looked up to see Joe the custodian looking nearly as surprised as she felt.

"Oh, Mrs. Burrows," he said, pulling the headphones of an ancient Walkman down off of his ears. "I'm so sorry, I didn't think anyone was in here." He awkwardly gestured to a stack of toilet paper on his cart. "I was just going to freshen up the bathroom. I can come back, though."

"Thanks so much," Cee-cee said cheerily, trying to keep the wobble out of her voice. "I was just dropping something off and needed to leave Nate a quick note. I'll be out of your hair in, like, five minutes?"

"Sounds fine," he said with an easy smile.

"Good to see you again, Joe."

"And you, Mrs. Burrows." He backed his cart up, closed the door, and headed down the hall.

She sat back on the leather chair and blew out a shaky breath.

Too close for comfort. She grabbed a sheet of paper and a

pen and scrawled out a quick note to Nate, thanking him for dinner, and then made her way to the bookshelf. Four minutes and thirty seconds to find something.

But as she continued her quest, pawing through the contents of the cabinet below the open shelves, she grew more and more discouraged. So far? *Nada.*

She opened the second cabinet and Cee-cee froze in surprise as she flipped over a framed photo and found herself staring at an image of herself and the kids. It was an old one. Max and Gabe looked to be about eight and ten. Did Nate have more of a sentimental streak than she'd thought?

No, not possible. He'd cast her aside too easily. Surely, he'd just tossed the old photo in his junk drawer and never bothered to take it out of the frame to replace it.

Then again, what would he replace it with? A professional portrait of his car?

She set the picture back in its place and pressed on, to no avail. Not even a scrap of mail. No print-outs from the doctor's office. None of the easy, incriminating evidence she'd hoped to find. This was nothing like Murder She Wrote, and she was no Angela Lansbury. What a stupid scheme.

What was she going to tell Max? *"Everything's fine with Daddy, don't worry about it"*?

Cee-cee snorted. Yeah, then distract her with some brownies and cartoons. Max wasn't five anymore. Distraction techniques wouldn't fly.

She turned her attention back to the desk and groaned. Blank paper, paperclips, pens. Not a single personal item. Nate Burrows, poised, neat, and professional, always.

This was useless.

God, Anna was going to kill her for this. As she put

everything back the way she'd found it, she racked her brain for something that might appease her sister.

Free cupcakes for life.

Wait, she already had that. A cupcake named after her? The Anna Banana. Banana bread cupcakes with praline frosting—

A sudden thought occurred to Cee-cee and she moved to stand behind the desk again. There was no way it could be that easy...Surely, a successful businessman like Nate wasn't using the same tired, old password?

She sat down in Nate's oversized leather chair and shook the mouse to life. The screen in front of her lit up, and she gave it a try. The make and year of that stupid car he loved so much.

The PC whirred and clicked, and, a second later, the desktop loaded.

Open tabs and all.

Eureka.

Blood pounded in her ears as she scanned the tabs on his web browser. Most were for local real estate listings. Not business, though, she realized with a start.

Residential.

Beach houses in the neighborhood of the house they'd built on the bay-front.

What in the world? Was he thinking of buying another house? That seemed so strange. Cee-cee hadn't loved the hard lines and sleek surfaces of the beach house, but that place had been built to Nate's exact specifications. He was crazy about it. She could understand if he were replacing their family house with something smaller, but all of these places were the same size as his current place. So why—

And then she saw it. An open email from a local realtor.

Here are the comps you requested. I think we could easily get a cool mil for your place in the current market.

He wasn't looking to buy a new house. He was looking at similar properties to see how much he could get for *his* house.

Cee-cee clicked over to the front page of Nate's emails and scanned the subject lines. Most were innocuous and work-related, a few spam, but one from Credit Karma caught her eye.

Looks like your credit score has dropped. Log in now to find out why, and how to fix it!

She scrolled down and spotted several past-due notifications. She let out a squeak as she realized one of them was for his *car*. His pride and joy, no dogs allowed, passcode to his computer car. Which could mean only one thing.

Nate was flat broke.

Cee-cee sat back, mind reeling. How had this happened? She couldn't imagine, but there was no time to think on it long. She quickly scrolled down a bit further through his emails, but, after a few moments, found nothing else of interest. Some automatic notices from a dating site, that was kind of sad, but nothing else.

A glance at the clock confirmed it was already two minutes past the time for Joe's scheduled return. She logged out of the computer and made sure that everything in and on Nate's desk was exactly as he'd left it, with the notable addition of a slightly crumpled box of cupcakes. Raspberry chocolate was his favorite.

Distant, tender moments flashed through her head, and she felt a surge of pity for the foolish man who had fathered her children.

Oh, Nate. What have you gotten yourself into?

Feeling no better than when she had started, Cee-cee left Nate's office and went to rescue Anna. The fixed smile she had used before came back so naturally that Cee-cee felt a wave of remorse for the decades of her life that she had worn that smile as a mask. No matter. She had created a new life for herself. So had Max, and Cee-cee wasn't going to let Nate shake that. Gabe and Sasha had *literally* created a new life, and she wasn't about to let Nate's worries weigh on them, either. She didn't know how, yet, but she would shield her children from his mistakes somehow.

Cee-cee found Sam's office, where that greased gorilla was standing entirely too close to her sister.

"Sorry to steal Anna away so soon," Cee-cee lied through bared teeth, "but I didn't realize the time! We're going to miss our lunch reservation if we don't head out right now."

"Oh, that's too bad." Sam looked genuinely disappointed, but then brightened. "I already ate, but I can join you if—"

"Nope. No, thank you!" Anna said quickly, ducking behind Cee-cee. "Wish we could, but our reservation is for two. New place, very French, very hard to get in. Bye!"

"I'll call you sometime! Your number is in the book?"

Anna was already out the door, leaving Cee-cee standing there, still smiling.

"Yes! It's in the book! Sorry, gotta run!" And she did, breaking into a jog. Thank God she didn't wear heels anymore.

By the time she caught up with Anna in the parking lot, they were both laughing hysterically.

"He is the woorrst," Anna said on a groan, drawing out the word. "You owe me."

"I do," Cee-cee agreed. "Lunch is on me."

"That's a *start*," Anna grumbled.

"Did you get any intel?" Cee-cee asked as they climbed into the car.

"Tons," Anna said, deadpan. "Sam has a yacht and a Rolls. He's excellent at archery, has the best wine cellar in Bluebird Bay, and he can bench — oh, I don't know, it was some impressive number. Unless his personal trainer is lifting it for him on the sly, or giving him dummy weights, that was definitely a lie. And also, he has some art he wants to show me."

Cee-cee chuckled, shaking her head as Anna started the car. "Did you find out anything about *Nate*?"

"Are you kidding? That would entail Sam talking about anything other than himself for a full minute. No chance. I tried to steer the conversation towards Nate, but Sam was too busy trying to make a move on me to notice. How about you? Please tell me you found something," she begged, "because I feel so dirty, I'm going to need to take three showers tonight."

"Well, rejoice, because I did find out a few very interesting nuggets about Nate. First off, he's flat broke. I don't know if it's just his personal finances or if the company's involved, but it's bad."

"No way," Anna exclaimed. "Nate? Money-is-my-life, have-you-seen-my-car, if-you-have-to-ask-you-can't-afford-it, *Nate*?"

"Overdue bills, sinking credit scores... he's selling the house, Anna."

"But he *loves* that stupid house. As much as he's capable of loving anything," she muttered. "So, what now?"

"I don't know," Cee-cee replied with a shrug. "I have to think about it."

She just had so many questions, none of which she could ask Nate without starting a fight.

Was this a new development, or was this something he'd been going through for a while now? Couldn't be that long. They had laid everything on the table with their divorce. But how had he gotten in so deep, so quickly? Cee-cee thought of the grim man that they had run into at the bar and shuddered.

One thing was for sure. There was more to this than she had turned up so far, and now that she was on the scent, she was going to see it to the bitter end.

Like she told her sister...She had no love for Nate Burrows, but she had nothing but love for the children he gave her. And if she had to have a knockdown, drag out battle to get him to tell her what the hell was really going on, she'd do it.

Put up your dukes, buddy boy, she thought grimly. *Cee-cee is ready to rumble.*

TODD

A MIX of anticipation and trepidation ran through him as he climbed the steps to Auntie Louise's cottage. The mess inside was a nightmare, and he didn't have a whole lot of confidence in his abilities as a parrot whisperer. But Alice had been on his mind constantly. Her smile haunted him, and her laugh...

Todd raised his hand and rang the bell.

He grinned like a fool when Alice opened the door, but her expression was more serious. A little crease sat in the space between her eyebrows, and her welcoming smile was tinged with worry.

"Reporting for duty," Todd said. "As promised. Do you like coffee? Or chai?" He proffered the two cups he had picked up on the way. "I wasn't sure, so I got one of each..."

Stop talking, Todd, he scolded himself silently.

"Thanks for coming, Doc." Like her expression, her voice was a mixture of welcome and worry. "I like both. Can I have the chai?"

"Of course." Todd handed it over.

"Thank you."

"Hey, look at this place!" Todd exclaimed as he crossed the threshold. He was pleasantly surprised to see how much of the trash Alice had cleared. The stacks of newspapers and magazines were gone, along with the calcified bird droppings. There were still piles of boxes and junk everywhere, but standing in Louise's living room no longer felt like being buried alive at the dump.

"Yeah, thanks," Alice said in a tired voice. She took a sip of her chai and seemed to perk up a bit. "Hmm, so good, thank you."

"Best in town," Todd told her. "The White Raven on Main. They make their own blend. I think it has orange peel in it? Nothing like bagged chai. I wasn't sure about dairy, or soy, so I got the macadamia milk. That one's my favorite."

Seriously...shut up, Todd.

"It's delicious." Alice savored another sip, then crinkled her nose as she looked around the living room. "Yeah, I spent two days clearing out all the stuff that was obviously trash. There's still a ton — and I think I'm being literal when I use that word – a *ton* of stuff to sort through. I don't want to throw away anything that's really precious to her, or even the stuff that could be donated to shelters and rummage sales and stuff, you know? I hate throwing stuff away."

"You've made amazing process. No wonder you look exhausted."

Why would you say that? demanded the persistent, annoying voice in his head.

But she just grinned at him. "I mean, yeah, it was a lot, but I actually feel better about the house now that there aren't towers of old news and bird poop everywhere."

She met Todd's eyes, and he saw the despairing sort of worry reappear.

"Barnaby is pulling out his feathers again," she told him. "Or they're falling out, I don't know. But he has a new bald spot on the other side now. I feel terrible. I'm failing him, and I'm failing my auntie. I thought hoarders were supposed to be obsessed with their stuff, but she doesn't even care about the house. Every time I visit or talk to her, all she asks about is Barnaby. I can't bring myself to tell her that he's not doing well. I just tell her that I've been giving him fresh fruit, and there's a vet coming to the house to make sure he's okay. She seems satisfied with that for now."

Alice managed a smile, but there were tears in her eyes. Todd felt an urge to take her in his arms and tell her that everything would work out, but he settled on a quick squeeze of the shoulder.

"You're doing a great job, and we're not giving up on him. Let's go take a look at the old boy."

Alice nodded and led him through to the kitchen.

"Big bucks, no whammies!" said the great green macaw as he caught sight of them.

"Well, he seems to be in decent spirits," Todd said.

"He's learning that I feed him when he talks," Alice told him. "He's screaming a lot less."

"That's major progress."

"But his feathers," Alice said sadly. "Look."

"Deal, or no deal?" Barnaby demanded.

Alice went to open the fridge as Todd stepped closer to examine the bird. Barnaby didn't look *too* bad, but Alice was right. There was another small bare patch opposite the first one. Alice stepped up next to him and popped an apple slice between the bars of the cage. Barnaby grabbed it before it even hit his bowl.

"You are the weakest link," he said cheerfully, holding the apple slice in one foot. "Goodbye!"

Alice popped another slice into his bowl.

"You two seem to be getting along better, at least," Todd said.

"Yeah," Alice said, but her tone was flat. "But I'm pretty sure despite the fact that he's liking the food options, he's still miserable without Auntie Louise here."

"So what can we do to make things better for now?" he asked, glancing around the place. "Your aunt clearly let him out a lot, and toys can only go so far. He needs to get out of that cage as soon as you feel confident he won't hurt you."

Alice wet her lips and nodded, her face a mask of guilt. "I know it's not like he's going to murder me or something. I was just really nervous. Since you've been coming, I've wanted to try to let him out, you know...but I was also afraid I wouldn't be able to get him back in and he might fly into one of the windows when I wasn't around or get into something dangerous."

"I totally get it and agree. She was lucky he didn't eat something that could've hurt him. But now that a couple of the rooms are mostly cleared out, let's see if we can finish the job in one of them. Then it will be safe to try it out in a confined area. He seems to trust us both a little..." Todd picked up the training stick that he had brought on his last visit, and Alice eyed the flimsy stick dubiously.

"He's not supposed to sit on that, is he?"

Todd grinned. "No, it's a target stick. You train him to follow it. You can use it to direct his beak away from your hands and face when you open the cage, and eventually you can use it to lead him back into his cage when you're ready to leave. It will help if you continue to feed him in his cage, including giving him most of his treats while he's in there. We'll start with the stick training for a couple days," he said, handing it over. "You don't even have to open the cage yet."

Alice raised one perfect eyebrow, looking dubious.

"You just put the stick near the cage. If he's curious — and parrots, especially bored parrots, are generally curious — then he'll move to touch it with his beak. When he does, you can say a reinforcement word, like *Good!* Some people use a clicker, but clickers can get lost. I think voice commands are better. After that, you give him a treat. And repeat. Eventually, he'll learn that following the stick earns him a reward."

"Sounds easy enough," Alice said, straightening her spine and nodding. She grabbed more apple slices from the fridge, which got Barnaby's attention.

"Step right up!" he said.

Alice stuck the target stick through the bars of the cage, a good foot from Barnaby's head. He shuffled over to inspect it, and as soon as his massive black beak brushed against the stick, Alice said, "Good boy!" and replaced it with a treat.

"You're a natural," Todd told her. Up close, he noticed that Barnaby's nails were overgrown and viciously sharp. One of them was ragged and broken — probably from tearing apart that parrot piñata Todd had supplied. Inwardly, he kicked himself for not paying better attention.

"Keep doing that," he told Alice. "See if you can get him

to move around the cage. I'll be right back — I just need to grab something from the car."

Todd ran out to his Jeep and grabbed a pair of doggie nail clippers. When he returned, Alice was successfully leading Barnaby around his cage with the target stick. She fed him the last apple slice and turned around to see Todd watching her.

"He's so smart, isn't he?" she marveled, looking a lot happier than she had when he'd first walked in. "He understands. Do you think my auntie did this with him?"

"Maybe," Todd said. "But macaws are really fast learners. I think the main thing here is to continue to build trust, both ways. Unfortunately, I need to do something that Barnaby won't like. I just hope it doesn't set us back."

Alice frowned at him. "What?"

Todd held up the nail clippers. "I need to trim those talons. When a parrot's nails are overgrown, they can injure themselves. If they break a nail, it can start to bleed. And then there's the fact that you don't want to interact with a bird who can draw blood by accident."

"No," Alice agreed, and said under her breath, "I only want to interact with a bird who can draw blood on purpose."

"Do you have a towel I can use?"

Alice gave him another raised-eyebrow look, but she proffered a clean kitchen towel without question. With smooth, slow movements, Todd opened Barnaby's cage and wrapped a towel around the bird's wings. The macaw was so surprised that he didn't fight or cling to his cage as Todd lifted him out. Holding him firmly and staying clear of the bird's massive beak, Todd quickly trimmed his nails. It was the same as trimming a dog's claws. A little bit at a time, mind the quick... done.

Todd was sorely tempted to let the bird roam the house, but they weren't ready for that. Barnaby's wings weren't clipped, and he could easily decide to go to the top of the wardrobe or a towering stack of boxes and refuse to come down. They'd have to go slow and steady. Todd set the bird back in his cage. When he closed the door, Barnaby finally protested the indignity with an ear-rending squawk.

"I'm sorry," Todd told the bird with sincere sympathy. "We'll get you out of there for a while real soon. I promise."

"That was amazing," Alice breathed. "You soothed the savage beast."

She winced as Barnaby screeched again.

"For a minute." She walked up to the cage and touched the training stick to the far side. Barnaby immediately climbed over to her. The instant he touched his beak to the training stick, she said, "Good boy!" and handed him a Brazil nut through the bars.

Todd found the last of the toys that he had purchased for Barnaby and put them in the parrot's cage. Barnaby muttered a rude phrase as Todd closed the door.

"I'll see if I can find him a concrete perch," Todd said to Alice. Her wide, dark eyes scrambled his thoughts, and he turned back to the macaw. "If he has enough materials to wear down his nails and beak, we won't need to keep trimming them. Since he's spending all of his time in that cage, he'll need more perches of different diameters to keep his feet from getting sore. That might be part of why he's been so ornery. Aside from boredom, sitting on that one perch all day can hurt his feet."

"I had no idea," Alice said remorsefully.

Todd touched her shoulder and then quickly dropped his hand.

"Neither did I," he said lightly. "I've been reading up on macaws."

"You have, haven't you?" She groaned. "Todd, you have a practice to run," she said, guilt carving a line across the smooth expanse of her forehead yet again. "We're taking up too much of your time."

"You're not," he said. When she looked unconvinced, he continued, "I promise. Learning on the job is part of it, especially now when I'm starting out. There's always more to know, and I never want to stop chasing answers down for my patients. That time is never wasted. It makes me a better vet. And I want to help. Both of you."

Alice grinned, and it was like the sun shining through the clouds. Her eyes seemed to get lighter, from black to a rich shade of amber. No, that was just the light slanting through the windows.

Keep it together, man.

He turned back to Barnaby.

"I can order him some new perches online," Alice said.

"Yeah..." Todd said, thinking. "And I can ask my brother to build Barnaby a training perch. According to Doctor Ketterman the First, Jeff's well on his way to becoming a master craftsman. I think he'd love an unusual project like that."

"She must be so proud of both of you," Alice said.

Todd's heart beat a strange staccato at a glimpse of her smile, and he turned his attention back to the bird.

"We'll give Barnaby somewhere to hang out when he's

outside of the cage," he said mechanically, "and give him treats when he's on it. That should make it easier to call him back if he goes somewhere you can't get to. For now, keep going with the target training every day. Maybe the next time I come, we'll bring him out and let him stretch his wings."

"Poor Barnaby," Alice said sympathetically, and sighed.

"I'd like to phone a friend," Barnaby told her, and she handed him another nut.

"Do you..." she began before breaking off. She cleared her throat and turned to face Todd. "Did you still want to help me with my treasure hunt? I understand if you're too busy—" she said quickly, but Todd cut her off.

"That's what I'm here for."

She grinned at him, but there was a skeptical slant to her brow.

"Really," he assured her. "All I've done for months is run the clinic. I haven't had time for anything else, including the gym. I'll consider it my work out for the day."

"This is a weird pick for your free time," Alice said cheerfully, "but I'll take it. We can start with these boxes."

A stack of fresh, flat moving boxes stood against the wall in the kitchen.

"I want to take any of the nicer clothes that don't fit auntie to the women's shelter. Trash can go in those bags there. Any of the other stuff that's worth saving, Auntie Louise said that I can take to her church for the rummage sale. She admitted that she has some money hidden away but doesn't remember where... so any money that we find, or anything valuable that I can sell, those go towards her care. We have to be very careful about what we throw away," Alice said as her face grew serious again. "I spoke to her for a long time yesterday, actually," she told him as she assembled the moving boxes. "I'm a little worried about how she's going to react when she realizes exactly how much stuff is gone. But honestly, my biggest regret is that we didn't step in before it got to this point."

"You're here now. Most people wouldn't do all this for their aunt."

She shrugged. "She's family. You do what you've gotta do. She knows what I'm up to, in theory, and agreed it's for the best—especially since her fall was a direct result of this mess. But I think she's going to be in shock when she sees what the house looks like. She said she wants pictures..."

Todd clapped his hands together and rubbed. "Well, let's try to make it look really great. That way, she can get a lot of money for the house and it will all be worth it."

Her brow smoothed and she beamed at him. "Sounds like a plan."

They worked for the rest of the day, focusing their attention on the biggest room in the house; the living room. It was dusty, heavy, dirty work, but Todd couldn't remember the last time he enjoyed himself so much. They tried to beat each other to the punch answering questions from the old game shows that Alice left playing for Barnaby, and held up different random items they'd unearthed and marveled at them.

As the hours passed, they managed to fill the new dumpster nearly a third of the way, Alice's car was packed to the brim with clothes and other items to donate, and Todd had loaded his Jeep with stacks of old books to bring to Max's bookshop to see if she wanted to buy them. The living room looked like...well, a living room, complete with dusty antique furniture that was clear enough to sit on.

Alice slumped onto the corner of the red, velvet couch and let out a satisfied sigh.

"Wow."

Todd perched on a gold armchair across from her and nodded. "Wow is right."

His muscles ached, but in a good way and he chuckled. "I was mostly kidding before, but this is way better than the gym. I'm sore in places I didn't even know had muscles."

"Right?" Alice grinned and flexed one trim arm to show off her biceps. "I'm going to be ripped by the time I'm done here."

Todd leaned forward and examined the contents of the scarred, old coffee table between them.

"Ready?" he asked, raising a brow at her.

"Let's do it," she agreed, leaning forward, as well.

The first hour of the day, they'd stopped each other a dozen times or more to show one another different cool things they'd found. Another small pile of stocks, a brooch that looked antique, and hats from the 1940s, still in their vintage hat boxes, never worn. Once they both realized that they were killing their momentum by stopping every five minutes, they made a pact to put anything interesting on the coffee table to go through at the end of the day.

Now, the two of them stared at the pile before them.

"You go first," Alice said, nodding at Todd. "What was your best find?"

Todd rifled through the pile and pulled out a stack of letters, tied together with frayed twine.

"I almost chucked them because they were wedged inside

a pile of magazines, but I remembered what you said and really went through everything as carefully as I could. They are postmarked anywhere from nineteen sixty-three to nineteen sixty-five," Todd explained as he handed them to Alice. Their fingers brushed, and a sizzle ran through him as his gaze collided with hers.

God, she was beautiful.

He cleared his throat and pushed on. "I didn't want to read them out of respect for Aunt Louise, but I'm sure she would appreciate them. This fell out of one of the envelopes."

He pulled a pressed, red rose from his t-shirt pocket and held it out to Alice.

"I bet they were from my uncle," she said as she took it gingerly from his hand. "He was in Vietnam around that time. They weren't married yet, and she waited for him to come home..."

Her eyes went suspiciously glassy and she blinked hard before taking a deep breath.

"I think she's going to be really happy when I bring them to her. I have to admit, it puts a lot of pressure on me, because my best find might not be anything at all," she said with a lopsided grin.

She set the letters and the rose reverently back on the table and reached for an old aspirin bottle.

He cocked his head and nodded. "Okay, I *am* pretty sore, so I'm not going to question it."

She barked out a laugh. "No, silly. Check it out." She popped the top off and turned it upside down onto her palm. A moment later, she held out her hand. He stared down at a gold ring with a red, square-cut gemstone in the center, surrounding by what looked like tiny diamonds.

CHRISTINE GAEL

He let out a low whistle. "Wow."

"Is it a real ruby, do you think?" she asked, extending her hand toward him.

He bent closer to examine the ring. "I'm definitely no expert, but it looks like one to me."

"It's stamped 14 karat gold, so there's a chance..."

"I know a place in town where you could get it checked out," Todd replied. "There is a jewelry store right near my aunt's cupcake shop. They do appraisals and buy antique jewelry. Otis Phipps owns the place, and he's said to be very fair."

"Maybe we can take it there together one evening after you get out of work, and have a cupcake while we're at it?"

Alice looked around for a safe spot to put the ring, and settled for sliding it on her finger.

"We could go tonight if you wanted?" he asked hesitantly.

She shook her head. "Nah. There is a lot of jewelry, and I know we're sure to find more. I think we should wait until we're done."

She must've seen his disappointed expression because she winced and cleared her throat. "I mean until *I'm* done. Don't think I'm expecting you to be doing this all the time now." Before he could correct her assumption and let her know he was only disappointed that he wouldn't get to spend more time with her tonight, she bit her lip and then continued in a rush. "Oh! And I also found $437 dollars under the mattress, $33 in a spice jar, and $700 in a fake soup can."

Todd stood to stretch and shot her a grin. "That's awesome!"

Alice shrugged. "To be fair, Auntie Louise told me about the soup can. She said that the money inside was for me for my hard work. I was thinking it would be a hundred bucks or something. Seven hundred dollars is a lot of money."

"The amount of time and effort you've put in? No one but family would do that. You've earned it," Todd said firmly, and Alice smiled.

"And so have you. I'm going to use most of this cash to get these wood floors cleaned and stained, but I think there is enough to buy us dinner, too. Auntie's treat. What do you say?"

A warmth spread through him, and he realized just how much he was dreading going home to his empty condo.

"I would love to," he replied sincerely. With a glance at his dust-covered clothes, he said, "But I could do with a bit of cleaning up, first."

"Me too. What say we meet up somewhere in an hour or two?"

"Perfect."

"Where should we go? I haven't been out since I came to town. It's been nothing but takeout and groceries."

"Bay Bar and Grill?" Todd suggested. "They have amazing wings."

"No whammies!" Barnaby shouted from the kitchen.

"Maybe don't mention 'wings' around the bird," Alice said with mock solemnity.

Todd threw up his hands in mock surrender and smiled. He glanced at his watch.

"Bay Bar and Grill?" he said again. "Seven o'clock?"

"See you there," Alice said with a brilliant smile.

Todd went out the front door and cleared the porch steps

in a single bound. This wasn't a date. He didn't have time to date. This was just two friends going out for a meal.

But his own reassurances didn't silence that little voice in his head that squawked almost as loud as Barnaby...

Liar.

13

TODD

Freshly shaven, showered, and wearing a clean collared shirt, Todd walked down the street with a kick in his step. He had plenty of time before he needed to head down the pier to Bay Bar and Grill, so he took an impromptu detour towards Mr. Bonomo's flower shop. It was nearly closing time, but he made it just under the wire.

"Hey, Todd!" Mr. Bonomo greeted him with a wide smile. "So good to see you. What can I do for you this evening?"

"Hello, Mr. Bonomo," Todd said, somewhat surprised by the enthusiastic greeting. He'd been in the shop a few times over the years to get his mom flowers on Mother's Day, but other than that, he didn't know the man all that well. "Time for one last bouquet before you close up shop?"

"For you? Always! Whose special day is it? It's not your mom's, I know that. And your cousin Max's birthday, I have that one on my calendar. All the shop owners in this plaza get a yellow rose for their birthdays, you know. Your Aunt Anna, then? She'd love this hellebore, take a look. I have a spotted pink one, and one so dark purple it's nearly black."

"Actually, none of the above," Todd said as a flush crept up his cheeks. Suddenly, he found himself wishing he hadn't shaved off the several days' worth of stubble that might've acted as camouflage. "They're for my date tonight."

"You don't say!" Mr. Bonomo beamed. "What sort of flowers does she like?"

"I'm not sure, but she loves bright, cheery colors. Yellow, orange, that sort of thing."

"I have plenty of flowers that fit the bill. I'd head over to that corner. There are tiger lilies, and black-eyed Susans, and loads of other wildflowers to choose from. Take your time and pick what you like. I have some bookkeeping to do anyhow. See what stands out to you, and then I can arrange them into a gorgeous bouquet."

"Sounds good, thanks."

Todd wandered over to the corner Mr. Bonomo mentioned and began choosing the flowers that he thought Alice would like. By the time he was done, he had put together a veritable riot of color that was as bright and dynamic as Alice. He brought the oversized bouquet up to Mr. Bonomo and shot him a quizzical glance.

"Well...what do you think?"

"Perfecto!" the florist exclaimed. "Let me balance it out with some lemon leaf and a few greens here, and it's going to be a showstopper."

Quickly but masterfully, the older man added touches of green that set the whole bouquet off. Then, he held it up for inspection.

"Looks great," Todd said.

"Agree! If you ever tire of surgery and shots, you're welcome to join me here at the shop."

"Thanks," Todd said, chuckling. "It's always good to have a backup plan."

"Actually, on that note..." Mr. Bonomo said as he wrapped the flowers, "I wondered if you could take a moment to look at my cat? Really, it would just take a minute, I think."

Todd's heart sank, but he tried not to let it show.

Why tonight?

"Of course," he found himself replying. "What's ailing...?"

"Bellflower," Mr. Bonomo supplied. "We call her Bell, for short. Well, her vet told us that she has diabetes. But he was in and out of the room in such a rush, I didn't have time to ask him any questions. Then, when I called this morning, no one called me back. I'm terrified to give her a shot and I'm terrified *not* to. Let me find Bellflower and the test strips and you can take a look at her."

Todd surreptitiously checked his watch as Mr. Bonomo headed into the back room. If he made the exam quick, and jogged down the pier—

"Here she is," Mr. Bonomo said, plopping a massive grey cat onto the counter.

"Hey there, Bellflower," Todd said softly, scratching the cat's head. She was overweight, but her coat was healthy, and she showed no signs of chronic dehydration.

"Do you have non-absorbent litter?" he asked.

Mr. Bonomo blinked. "What's that?"

"You'll need to switch at least one litter-box over to something that won't absorb Bell's urine. You can buy a commercial non-absorbent litter or use something like aquarium gravel. Then, when she goes to the bathroom you can just stick the glucose strip into a puddle. If there's glucose in the urine, it's safe to give her a dose of the insulin that your vet gave you."

"How, um, how do I do that?"

Todd was shocked.

"The vet didn't show you?" he asked.

"He said the directions were on the box," Mr. Bonomo said, "but then I had no way to catch her 'in the act' so to speak."

"The new litter will fix that problem. I'd give her a shot right now, but we'll have to wait until you have the chance to test her urine, just to be safe."

"I'll stop on my way home tonight. And if her sugar is high, I do the shot?"

The florist's brow was still furrowed with worry, and Todd pushed aside the urge to check his watch again.

"I can give you a quick primer on insulin injections, if you like. Your insulin is in the fridge, right?"

"Yeah, it said that on the bottle."

"Good. The dose should be on the bottle, too. So, you mix it by rolling it between your hands." Todd illustrated with a cut stem from the counter. "Never shake it, or you'll create bubbles. You know how to fill the syringe?"

"Yeah, I can do that. Upside-down, no air bubbles."

"Exactly. So, it's best to give her the injection right after she eats. Did your vet talk to you about her diet?"

"No, not a word."

Todd groaned internally.

"Write these down." Mr. Bonomo quickly grabbed a pen

and paper as Todd rattled off some options for new foods. "That last one is basically just freeze-dried meat. It's much healthier than kibble."

"Thank you so much, Todd. You're a lifesaver, and you just earned yourself a new patient. Not even her doctor spent that much time explaining to me," the older man said, his eyes glassy with gratitude. "The flowers are on the house. Go on, get out of here. Don't leave that girl waiting."

"Thanks!" Todd said with a quick grin, already hustling toward the door.

If not for fear of ruining Alice's flowers, he would've sprinted to the restaurant. Instead, he settled for speed walking down the pier, dodging the few people strolling along. When he finally arrived at Bay Bar and Grill, Alice was sitting alone at a table. In spite of his guilt, he had to grin when he caught sight of her outfit. Lemon-yellow jeans, a purple sweater, and a chunky orange necklace. She matched her bouquet perfectly.

"I am so sorry," he said the moment she spotted him. "I thought I had time to stop for flowers, but then the florist wanted me to look at his diabetic cat—"

His explanation was cut short as Alice burst out laughing.

"Well, that's either true or the best dang excuse for being late in the history of mankind, so either way, I'll give you a pass," she quipped, reaching out to accept the flowers.

Todd let out a sigh of relief and slumped into the table across from her. She touched the bouquet to her nose and grinned.

"This is the most perfect bouquet I've ever seen in my life. I love it. Thank you."

"I'm glad you like it," Todd said, smiling like an idiot.

"And *I'm* glad you didn't bring me roses."

"Not a fan?" Todd laughed.

"I like them when they're on the bush, especially the English garden kind. But the mostly-closed, imported ones that smell like plastic? No thanks. But *these*," she said, turning her eyes back to the wildflowers she held in her hands before placing them carefully on the table, like they were something precious. "These are *amazing*."

"Mr. Bonomo has a great selection," Todd said.

"You'll have to take me there. Auntie's room is dreary. I'd love to make her a bouquet."

"It's a date," he told her. Alice grinned.

"Okay, so I had some time to look over the menu while I was waiting and I have a pretty important question to ask you." She leaned in, eyes bright with challenge and a hint of mischief. "Have you tried their Fight or Flight Challenge?"

"Their what?" Todd laughed, shaking his head.

"I'll take that as a no," said Alice cheerfully. "So, we get five rounds of wings, each hotter than the one before. They start off super mild, like the sweet sesame ones with just a hint of back-end spice, and they ramp up to the blow-your-skull-off, call the fire department hot. If you finish them all, you get a t-shirt."

"I'm in," Todd said with a solemn nod.

He couldn't lie. With her looking at him like that, he'd have agreed to almost anything, but this actually sounded like fun. After having one too many dates in the past with girls who wouldn't even order a chicken wing for fear of getting sauce on their face in front of a date, this only made him appreciate Alice's sense of adventure and fun even more.

Their waitress approached with a smile, and welcomed them to the restaurant.

"Before we order...sorry to be a bother, but any chance I could borrow a vase?" she asked, wrinkling her nose. "If I ruin these flowers, I'll never forgive myself."

"Wow, those are gorgeous!" their server said. "I don't think we have any vases that size, but how about a pitcher?"

"That would be perfect, thank you. And then, we're going to order your Fight or Flight wings."

"Brave woman," said the waitress approvingly. "And to drink?"

"I'll try a glass of your cranberry-apple cider, please."

"That's my favorite," the waitress said. She had clearly taken a liking to his date. "Are you new to town, or just visiting? I haven't seen you around. I would have noticed your style. Really cool."

Alice laughed. "I'm new to town," she said, and Todd's heart thumped.

Not just visiting?

"I knew it. I wasn't getting that tourist vibe, you know? My name is Sandy. If you're looking to meet new people our age, we're doing a girls' night at the bowling alley tomorrow? Might sound lame, but the place is basically a historical landmark. Plus, there's a grandma in the kitchen who makes *the* most amazing lobster bisque."

"That sounds really fun," Alice said.

"I'll drop my number before my shift ends and you can hit me up if you want to come. Gotta go, my manager's giving me the side-eye." Sandy turned to Todd with a smile. "Anything to drink?"

"I'll have the blonde IPA."

"Sounds good," Sandy said as she put his order into the handheld device that each of the servers carried. "I'll be back in a few."

She bounced over to the next table, where she continued talking with the same speed and enthusiasm.

"I remember when I had that much energy," Todd said with a sigh.

"Was it this morning before you lugged six tons of books from my Auntie's house?" Alice said with a laugh.

"I think it was before I went for my DVM," he quipped. "You going to go bowling with them?"

"Depends how much I get done tomorrow. She seems nice, and I wouldn't mind making some more friends."

"Come with me to the bookshop sometime soon," Todd said impulsively. "You'd love my cousin Max."

"Sure," she replied with a nod. "I'd love that."

Sandy breezed by with a pitcher full of water and their drinks. Alice carefully unwrapped her bouquet and placed it in the pitcher.

"A perfect fit!" she said happily.

They chatted easily for a few minutes before Sandy returned with the first round of wings and a second pitcher of water.

"You probably won't need this yet, and I've heard that water can make the burn worse, but I feel obligated to bring it," she said with a wink. "I wish you good luck," she added before backing away with an ominous laugh.

"I didn't even look at the menu to see," Todd said, eying the wings. "What are these first ones supposed to be?"

"Well, this one with the sesame seeds must be the sweet

sesame garlic. Which would make this other plate the maple glazed."

Todd's stomach growled and he snagged one of each.

He found the maple ones a bit too sweet, but he was all about the sesame garlic, while Alice liked both.

The next round featured two wings each of three pleasantly spicy varieties, honey barbeque, Cajun style, and whisky glazed. The spice built as they ate, and Todd ordered a second glass of beer.

"You're not tapping out already, are you?" Alice teased.

"Not a chance," Todd said.

Sandy set down a platter of massive wings dripping with a dangerous-looking red sauce, and Todd stared.

"What are *those*?"

"I believe these would be hot and spicy turkey wings, Doc." Her eyes widened as she took a bite.

"Too hot and spicy?" Todd asked.

She help up a finger as she chewed and then swallowed. "Nope. These are *the* most delicious wings I have ever tasted. I love turkey."

Todd almost invited her to Thanksgiving at his mother's house, then promptly stuffed a turkey wing in there instead. The thought, *Too soon, dummy,* was quickly replaced by *Jeez, these wings are hot.*

"Is this the final round?" he asked. Alice laughed.

"Nope."

"Then I'm going to need another beer at the ready," he murmured, signaling to Sandy.

"Are you sure you don't need a glass of milk?" Alice asked.

"No," he replied with as much dignity as he could muster. "An Imperial Stout should do the trick."

Alice drained the last of her cranberry cider and ordered another.

The fourth round, Korean barbeque, was on par with the hot and spicy. Eye-watering, but not so hot that he couldn't taste the ginger and garlic.

"That might have been my favorite so far."

"Nothing beats the turkey for me," Alice said.

"So, what's the final challenge going to be?"

"Turkey again," she said with a grin. "But these are Carolina reapers."

"What kind of name is that?" Todd laughed.

"An excellent one! It's the name of the pepper. It's a cross between a ghost pepper and a red habanero."

"Why do you know that?" he demanded.

"I may have an affinity for spicy cuisine," said Alice with a wink. Then she grinned. "My college had a yearly chili cook-off, and there was a prize for the hottest pot of chili. The catch was, the chef had to sit and eat a whole bowl of it to win. I won three years running."

"A woman of hidden talents."

"You know it." Alice grinned as the final two wings arrived at the table. "Warning: We have to clean those bones to win the t-shirt. Are you ready?"

"As I'll ever be."

"One..." Alice said, hand hovering over the plate.

"I feel like I need gloves," Todd muttered.

"Two..."

"My hands are my livelihood!" he protested in mock panic.

"Three!" She grabbed the turkey wing and tore into it with her perfect white teeth. Todd did the same and immediately regretted it.

"Oh wow, that's good!" she said between bites. "Kind of fruity."

"I taste nothing," Todd panted. "I feel nothing. I think my taste buds have been obliterated by the nuclear heat of that sauce."

"So it should be easy to finish!" Alice's tone was cheerful, but he could see her eyes watering. Tears streamed down his own cheeks as he powered through the ridiculously oversized wing, his upper lip was bathed in sweat by the time he finished.

He and Alice dropped their wings at the same time.

"Victory!"

"We did it!" Alice shouted, raising her saucy hands in victory. "Hey, Sandy! We did it! Bring on the t-shirts!"

"And milk!" Todd called, laughing in spite of the pain. Alice beamed at him and he knew his destroyed taste buds were entirely worth it.

Sandy appeared with t-shirts and wet wipes — but, unfortunately for Todd, no milk. His mouth was still burning as they cleaned their fingers. There was a paper cut on one finger that he hadn't noticed before; it felt like someone had taken a hot brand to his hand.

"Don't touch your eyes," Alice warned him cheerily.

"Not for a million dollars," Todd agreed.

Alice pulled off her purple sweater — she was wearing a bright orange tank top underneath — and immediately replaced it with an oversized shirt that read *I Survived the Bay Bar and Grill Fight or Flight Challenge!* over a picture

135

that showed a cartoon turkey and chicken with flames in place of wings.

"Don't wear that in front of Barnaby," Todd warned. "He's been watching game shows for longer than you've been alive. I'm pretty sure he can read."

"Not for a million dollars," said Alice in a pompous baritone.

"I do not sound like that," he protested.

"I think it was spot on," she said with a bubbling laugh.

"Should we move to the bar?" He was having a great time and wasn't ready to call it a night.

"Sure," said Alice agreeably. "It's closer to the band. I can hardly hear them over here."

Todd, who hadn't even noticed there *was* a live band, paid the bill despite Alice's protests and then followed her to her choice of seats. He ordered a coke and she a club soda from the server, and then faced the miniature stage.

"They're good," she said approvingly, nodding along to the music.

"Do you ever play anymore?" Todd asked. "Perform, I mean? With other musicians?"

"It's been a while. I didn't really play in college at all. I was so burnt out after high school that I told my mom to sell my instruments, but she just tucked them away in a closet. She even brought them with her when she moved back to Maine.

"I picked them up again after I graduated. Actually, I traded my violin in for a five-string fiddle. I met this musician as soon as I moved to Portland, and he convinced me to play in bars with him here and there. Cajun music mostly, stuff I'd never played before. It was fun, playing in places where everyone's laid back and having a good time."

"Are you..." Todd stopped himself from asking about this mystery musician. "Do you think you'll keep playing with the Cajun band, when you go back to Portland?"

"Not a chance. He cheated on me," Alice said shortly, eyes on the band.

"Oh," Todd said.

"*Oh*," Alice repeated with emphasis. She glanced at him and smiled. "But I would still like to play sometimes. In fact, I wouldn't mind playing a few gigs in Bluebird Bay. You know anybody who likes bluegrass?"

"I like bluegrass," said Todd, who had never heard a note of bluegrass music beyond the snippet that Alice had played on the fiddle she had found. It wasn't a lie, though. He'd loved it when she played it.

"Hmph," Alice said, but a smile played on her lips. She was still watching the band.

"Alice?" Todd said. She turned to look at him, and her luminous brown eyes made his pulse race. "Any man who would cheat on you is a complete and utter fool."

She blinked and then looked down at her hands.

"You're sweet," she said.

Todd reached out and placed his hand over hers.

"Do you know how long you're going to be in Bluebird Bay?"

"I'm not sure." Her hand moved tentatively against his, thumb running lightly over the back of his hand. "There's so much more work to do at Auntie's place."

"I can come over after work," Todd offered, shoving away

the nightmare images of his schedule that flashed through his head. "Maybe not tomorrow, but the next day?"

"Todd...it's a lot... Are you sure?"

"I wouldn't have offered if I wasn't sure. I want to see what other treasure we can dig up." He squeezed her hand. "The company's good, too."

Alice squeezed back. "It is."

For the next hour, they hung out, listened to music and chatted. The conversation flowed so easily that the time flew by. They played 'name the band' as various, familiar songs came on, and laughed as they shared first concert stories.

It was the best date he'd ever been on, and he hated for it to end.

"Would you like another?" he asked as Alice finished her drink.

"No, thank you," she said with a wince. "Actually, I really should get back home. I have an article to finish tonight before I go to bed and the plumber is coming to Auntie's early in the morning."

"Do you need a ride home?"

"I drove."

"I'll walk you to your car, then."

He did, and was disappointed to find it was only a dozen yards away.

"Thanks for inviting me," he said as they stood outside the driver's side door, "and for helping earn that t-shirt. I haven't had this much fun in ages."

"Thank *you*," she replied. "For the flowers," she said, holding them up, "and for the wings. The evening was supposed to be on Auntie."

"You can take me out for cupcakes when we go to Max's

bookshop." No point in mentioning that if Aunt Cee-cee was there, the cupcakes would be free.

"You got it."

"Well," Todd said awkwardly, hands in his pockets as he tried to decide whether to kiss her or not. "Good night, Alice."

She nodded and then rolled onto her tiptoes to give him a quick kiss on the lips.

"Good night, Todd," she whispered.

If someone had told him two weeks ago that he'd be half in love with a dynamo who played the fiddle, handled spice like a champ, and argued with a snarky parrot named Barnaby, he'd have said they were nuts.

But as he stood there long after her car pulled away, grinning like a fool, he knew it was true.

He was crazy about Alice.

And she might not even be in town next month, he reminded himself with a wince.

Not only that, he didn't have the time to invest in a new relationship. Hell, he didn't have the time to even get a decent night's sleep most days. But as the very thought of not seeing her again came in like a dark, gray cloud covering the sun, he knew that he wasn't about to give her up.

Even if spending more time with her only made it all the worse when things didn't work out.

He turned on his heel and headed for his car, stomach roiling with acid in the aftermath of their wing-fest.

He truly must be a glutton for punishment.

14

CEE-CEE

CEE-CEE HELD a piping bag full of bright blue frosting — her homemade food coloring was a smash success, and it was as simple as boiling dried butterfly pea flowers in water for a few minutes before straining it and adding a quarter cup of the deep blue liquid to her vanilla frosting. Blue raspberry today; the cupcakes were filled with raspberry jam, and each one would get a sprinkle of freeze-dried raspberries on top.

Two trays of cupcakes sat waiting, but she found herself staring off into space instead of piping. Nate had texted her the day before to thank her for the cupcakes, and she had just replied *no problem.*

But it was all a problem.

A very big problem.

Should she call him to discuss what she had found? She had barely slept the past couple days, tossing and turning until she had finally come down to the basement at four in the morning to start the baking.

How could she possibly approach him without admitting what she had done and stirring up trouble? She could hardly believe that she had gone to his office to begin with. But she just couldn't shake the thought that Nate was in deep... something that went beyond overdue bills and a too-expensive house.

Who were those men in the bar? Was Nate in trouble with some gang? The mafia? The thought of either one existing in Bluebird Bay seemed ludicrous, and yet something about those men had set off alarm bells in Cee-cee's head.

She threw her piping bag down on the table and stripped off her apron.

Time to call in for backup, she thought as she picked up her phone.

Again.

It was good to have sisters who always had her back.

"Hey, Cee-cee," Steph said after the first ring.

"Steph, good morning. Do you have an hour or two to spare? I need some help down here. The cupcakes and the frosting are all made. I just need somebody to ice the cakes before the shop opens."

"Sure," her sister agreed. "I don't have another yoga class until after lunchtime."

"Thank you so much."

"Happy to help," Steph said cheerfully, "so long as I can snag a few cupcakes as payment."

"Always," Cee-cee replied.

"I'll be there within the hour."

"Thanks. I need to go, but Wanda will be upstairs. I'll leave the door unlocked."

"Sounds good," Steph replied. Thank goodness Stephanie was doing so well these days, Cee-cee thought as she hung up. One family crisis at a time, please and thank you.

She matched each bowl of frosting with its cakes and jotted down some instructions for her sister, then went upstairs to tell Wanda that Stephanie would be in to finish up. After that, Cee-cee got in her car and drove straight to Nate's office. Ten to one the man was already there, eating breakfast at his desk — if drinking an olive green protein shake could qualify as 'eating breakfast'.

When Cee-cee arrived at the commercial real estate office, she walked straight in, not giving herself time to second guess it.

"Hello, Denise," she greeted the receptionist. "Is Nate in?"

Before the woman could answer, Nate appeared from his office.

"Oh, hey, Celia," he greeted her with a puzzled smile. "Twice in one week. Is everything okay?"

"No," she said shortly, knowing she should play it cool in front of the clearly puzzled receptionist, but not quite being able to manage it. "Not really. Can we talk privately?"

"Of course," Nate said after a brief pause. "Come into my office."

Cee-cee followed him through and shut the door behind her. He perched on the edge of his desk, and she slumped into one of the chairs in front of it.

Just let it rip.

"I hacked into your computer," she blurted, and Nate stared at her in surprise. "That one. Right there," she added, jabbing a forefinger at the desktop.

"You *what?*" he said.

"I read your emails, and I saw the house listings. I saw the overdue notices, and I met these strange men at the bar, and—"

Get it together, Cee-cee, she thought in frustration. *Just ask the dang question.*

"Are you in debt with the mafia?"

Nate let out a short, humorless laugh. He walked around to the far side of his oversized desk and collapsed into his chair.

"When Denise said Anna had come with you and went off with Sam, I couldn't figure out what the hell she would be doing with him," he said. "I should have known you two..."

"Tell me what's going on," Cee-cee demanded. Belatedly, she added, "Please."

"Not the mafia, but yeah, I'm in debt. With people I never should've taken a loan from. When you... when we got divorced, I wasn't myself. Even before that, the decisions that I was making..." He shook his head. "I spent a lot of time regretting things that I'd done, wondering what I should have done differently. I didn't have my head in the game. I made a bad investment. A very bad one. When it tanked, I had to take out a loan with... let's say, 'less than ideal' terms. It's been a struggle to pay it back."

"How much?" Cee-cee asked, but he didn't seem to hear her.

"I have some great deals in the pipeline," Nate said, staring over her shoulder. "If I can get through the next six months, it will be okay. But the loan is due now. They're not willing to wait six months. I was hoping that I could just pound the pavement and get some deals done to bridge the gap, but you know how real estate is around the holidays."

She did. They had been married for thirty years, and she'd seen the ebb and flow of the real estate business. Between the holidays and construction slowing down for the winter, there was a dearth of action until things picked up again in the spring. A scary image ran through her mind and she winced.

"I don't know what to say, Nate. All I can picture is a severed horse head in your bed and our daughter weeping. What if these guys try to give you cement shoes? Feed you to the fishes."

Nate laughed again, and there was a slightly hysterical edge to it.

"I don't think it will come to that, but a busted knee or two isn't out of the question."

Cee-cee gasped.

"Sorry," he muttered. "Just kidding."

"It didn't sound like you were kidding," she said. "Nate, how much money are we talking about?"

"Five," Nate said, looking down at his desk. "Hundred."

"*Five hundred THOUSAND* dollars?" Cee-cee exclaimed. "Dear God, Nate. Why?" She paused, struggling to catch her breath. "How?"

Nate didn't reply. She took a deep breath and shook her head.

"I don't have anything near that amount. All of my profits have gone back into the business, into setting up the shops in Portland and Westbrook." She had savings set aside, but that was for emergencies. True emergencies, for her or the kids. Not self-inflicted emergencies created by her ex-husband. And even if she wanted to help him — and she had to admit that she did, if only for the sake of their children — her savings account didn't even approach that number.

He gave her a bemused look. "I know you don't."

Cee-cee leaned back.

"Then why were you buttering me up?" she asked. "I thought you wanted to ask me for a loan?"

"Nope," Nate said with a sad smile. "I was feeling sorry for myself. Everything else was so bad, and being around you makes me feel better. More stable. I think part of me hoped that part of *you* still loved me. And with you and Mick engaged, I didn't want to add even more regrets to my life by just letting you get married without at least telling you...or showing you how I felt." His cheeks flushed. "Sad, I know. I'm sorry. It's been a rough couple years."

"I'm sorry that you're having a hard time." She couldn't let herself get caught up in feeling bad for him about all that right now. It was in the past. They had much more pressing issues at hand and she rerouted the conversation back to them. "But we need to figure this out. What are you going to do, Nate?"

He shrugged helplessly. "I have a few more irons in the fire," he said in a listless voice. "And if the house sells soon, I can at least give them the few hundred thousand I have in equity. I'd have taken out a loan against it, but I ruined my credit by robbing Peter to pay Paul over the last six months, and they wouldn't give one to me."

"Okay," she muttered, gears grinding as she tried to think. "Nate, I know you're not meaning to cause her concern, but Max is worried about you," Cee-cee told him. "Will you talk to her?"

"And tell her what?" he shot back with a groan. "That, in

addition to being a complete failure as a family man, I'm an incompetent businessman?"

"Tell her that you're not dying," Cee-cee urged, and he looked up at her in surprise. "You've been acting so weird that we wondered if you'd gotten some terrible diagnosis."

"I'll talk to her," he said shortly. "It's not your problem, so please just forget it. I'll handle it."

He looked so pathetic that Cee-cee almost wanted to get up and comfort him, but it wouldn't do to send the man mixed signals when he'd had thoughts of stealing her away from her fiancé.

As *if*.

And yet, she couldn't just walk away.

"What is the real worst case scenario here, Nate?"

He blanched and wet his lips. "I think so long as I'm paying them something, it will be okay. I have more stuff I can sell. But if something doesn't come through for me in the next few months, they're going to get impatient. I might get roughed up a little for incentive."

She winced and let out a groan.

"They're not going to kill me. And I've always been just a little too handsome, anyway, so a missing tooth or scar might make me more approachable," he added with a crooked smile.

"Right." She shook her head slowly at his joke and blew out a sigh. "Okay. At least I know now. I'll try to think of some way to help," she insisted. "Though, I know this is more than a bake sale type of situation."

Nate shot her an affectionate smile she'd have killed to receive a couple years back.

"Thanks, Celia. Hey, do you want to stay for lunch? Your treat," he added with a chuckle.

"No. Thank you. I'll call you if I think of something. And you'll talk to Max?"

"I said I would, and I will," he told her, going to open the office door.

But Max would ask her regardless. How in the world was she going to explain this to her in a way that would make her worry less?

15

NIKKI

"This is my living nightmare," Beth grumbled. She was curled into a defensive posture in the passenger seat, arms crossed, head down, legs tucked up underneath her like there was a fair chance she might drop and roll from the moving car at any moment.

"We needed to get out of that apartment," Nikki said. "*You* needed to get out of that apartment."

"I hate bowling," her daughter groused.

"You love bowling."

"I liked it when I was, like, nine and I was going with my friends. Not as the third wheel on a date with my mom and her *man*-friend. If he's weird, I'm going to take the car and bail. You can't make me stay. I'm a legal adult."

Nikki let out something between a laugh and a sigh.

"Right," she said with forced cheer, "but you still live on my dime, and guess what? I pay the cost to be the boss."

"Ew," Beth groaned. "Shouldn't no dad jokes be one of the very few perks of not having a dad?"

Ouch.

The corny phrase *was* a dad joke. Nikki's dad's, specifically, and one he'd said to them all growing up, including Beth. The funny part was, Eric Merrill was a big, old softie who gave in on basically anything his kids and grandkids wanted, so the line was pretty much always said in jest. Despite Beth's snarky comeback, it seemed to have worked to lighten the mood, because she unfolded her arms and didn't look like she was on the edge of bolting.

Baby steps.

"I called him," she told her mother. "Grandpa, I mean."

"Oh yeah?" Nikki replied cautiously.

"I had to tell him that I wasn't staying in Bluebird Bay to, like, avoid him or whatever. I just wanted him to know that I'm not mad at him or anything. I came to meet Anna. And," she added grudgingly, "to make sure you were okay after everything that happened with my—um, with Steve."

"And?"

"He said he understood. You know Grandpa, he doesn't hold a grudge or make people feel bad for missing a holiday or anything. I could tell he misses us, though, so we've got to make sure we spend Christmas there."

"I miss him, too," Nikki said. Her older siblings, on the other hand, not so much. She pushed aside the guilt for not returning Jack's call. She'd done her duty and had texted Gayle the day before to confirm that they wouldn't be attending Thanksgiving. That announcement had been met with stony silence so far, which only solidified her feelings about all of this. The space from her two older siblings had been good for her.

It felt healthy.

When she got back to Cherry Blossom Point, there were

going to be some changes. Changes that were sure to cause a ruckus, but too bad.

She shelved those thoughts as Beth continued.

"He said since I'm already here, I might as well meet your new boyfriend. Check him out and make sure he isn't a serial killer or something."

Which explained why Beth hadn't fought her harder when she'd suggested coming tonight. She sent a mental high five to her dad.

She gripped the wheel tighter as Beth shot her a probing, sideways glance.

"Grandpa wanted to know if you're moving here for good."

"We still have our house in Cherry Blossom Point," Nikki replied.

"That's not an answer, Mom."

"No," she admitted. "It's not."

"So?"

"I don't know what the future will hold, Beth, but right now, I have no plans to do that. There is a lot to consider. You, your aunts and uncle, and Grandpa is getting older. No matter what, I *am* going home soon after you go back to school, though. Mateo and I are going to do long distance for a while. And then we're going to see what happens," she answered honestly. "Tonight is going to be a great first step. You can see what I've been doing here—"

"You mean *whom* you've been doing here," Beth muttered, but it was more teasing than bitter.

"Beth!" Nikki gasped on a laugh. "Ew!"

Her daughter cackled gleefully, and despite the reason for her chuckles, Nikki joined in.

"*What* I've been doing here," Nikki repeated, "and the people I've grown to care about."

"Okay, Mom. I'll do my best not to be a brat. But I've been feeling pretty emo, what with the attempted murder – suicide thing and all, so... no promises."

"Understood," Nikki said in a warm voice. "We can leave whenever you're ready. Just give it a chance, okay?"

"That's the plan."

She pulled into the parking lot and led Beth around to the front of the building, where a neon sign declared *Bowling and Soup* over an older wooden sign that read *Young's Bowling Alley*. Mateo was waiting for them just inside the front doors. He rose to greet them, giving Nikki a hug and a peck on her hairline before extending a hand to Beth.

"Hello, Beth. I'm Mateo. It's good to finally meet you."

Beth shook his hand and dropped it quickly.

"There's someone I'd like you to meet." Mateo gestured towards the kitchen in back. They followed him, and he called Judy Young up to the window. She beamed, wrinkles deepening, dentures flashing as she caught sight of Nikki.

"Welcome back!" she said with enthusiasm. "It's good to see you again."

"Hello, Judy," Nikki said with a smile. "This is my daughter, Beth."

"Well hello!" Judy said enthusiastically. "Do you like chowder, Beth, or are you more of a bisque girl?"

Beth smiled, charmed against her will. "I like both."

"I have a new soup I'm working on," Judy said as she stepped down from her kitchen-window stool and bustled over to her stovetop stool. "It's a crab bisque," she called over her shoulder. "Plenty of butter and garlic. I'm still trying to get the spices just right."

She popped up at the window and handed Beth a paper coffee cup.

"Thank you," Beth said, accepting the soup. Judy was watching expectantly, so she took a sip. Her eyebrows shot up. "Wow! This is delicious. It tastes like king crab legs dipped in garlic butter. Yum!" She took another sip and handed the cup to her mom. Nikki accepted it and drank, letting the warm, creamy bisque trickle down her throat.

"Wow," Nikki echoed. "This might be even better than the lobster one," she said earnestly.

"You don't think it needs a kick?" Judy asked.

"Nope. It's just perfect." Nikki took another sip, savoring it.

"Did you know my mom's a professional chef?" Beth asked.

"I did not!" Judy exclaimed. "Okay, Nikki. Chef to chef, tell me."

Nikki tasted the bisque one more time, with her eyes closed. "Seriously, it's perfection. Now, if you wanted to top it off with some crispy fried shallots as a garnish, I wouldn't kick it out of bed."

"Genius!" Judy declared, and turned to Mateo. "That's exactly what it needs. You've got a good one here. What about you, Matty? What will it be?"

"I'll have what she's having," he replied.

Judy brought them two more cups of the crab bisque.

"Thank you, Mrs. Young." He turned to Nikki and Beth. "Shall we?"

They swapped their boots for bowling shoes and claimed Mateo's favorite lane.

"Where are the screens?" Beth asked with a puzzled frown.

Mateo covered his laugh with a cough, and he was solemn when Beth turned to look at him.

"No screens here. We keep score the old fashioned way. Or not — we could just bowl."

Beth insisted that Mateo keep score... and then promptly bowled three gutter balls in a row.

"I haven't done this in, like, a decade, and I recall being a lot better at it," she muttered.

"And I seem to remember lane guards at most of those birthday parties," Nikki said.

"Want me to give you a couple of easy pointers?" Mateo asked Beth.

"Sure," she said with a shrug. "Why not."

"First," he said, selecting a teal blue ball off of the rack, "try this one instead. It's a little bit lighter, which means it's easier to control where you aim it."

"Okay," Beth said dubiously, accepting the bowling ball.

"Next is the approach race."

"The what?" Beth laughed, and it warmed Nikki's heart to watch them. Mateo was so warm and relaxed... the father she wished Beth could have had growing up.

"That's what serious bowlers call the little walk up to the line," he said with mock gravity. "You don't want to rush it, but you also don't want to stop or stall. You've been pausing at the line and pulling your body back, which throws everything off. You don't want to stop moving until after you've released the ball. It's one smooth movement, swinging your arm like a pendulum. Give it a try."

Beth walked, swung, and released all in one movement. The ball slid, rolled, curved, and then took out all but one of the pins with a satisfying *crack*. Beth shrieked in excitement and raised her hands in the air, turning around to face them.

"You're a natural!" Mateo said.

"That was amazing, Beth! You two keep playing and I'll be right back. That bisque was delicious, but I came in starving. Do you want a cup of chowder with sourdough?"

"Um, duh!" Beth said with a smile that made her heart squeeze.

"Mateo?" Nikki asked.

"I never say no to chowder. Thanks!"

"Back in a jiff," she said, and walked back to the kitchen.

"Mrs. Young?" she called through the window.

"Stop it," the old woman replied with a snort as she bustled across the kitchen, "Judy."

"Three bowls of clam chowder please...Judy," Nikki said.

"Sammy!" Judy called to a gangly teenager standing behind her. "You heard the lady. Three chowders."

"Coming right up, Gram."

"It's good to see you in here again," Judy said to Nikki. "Do you know that you're the first lady that our Matty has ever brought in here? Not counting his Tara, of course. He's been bringing her in since she was knee-high, just like his daddy did with him and his sister, Flora. He must like you a lot."

Nikki looked over to their lane, feeling warm to the tips of her fingers. Mateo and Beth were both sitting on the leather couch, heads bowed in serious conversation.

"I like him a lot, too," Nikki murmured.

"And you should!" Judy declared. "Matty's a gem. I should know, I had a good hand in raising him."

Nikki looked back to Mrs. Young. "You did?"

"What has he told you about his parents?" she asked in a low voice.

"I know about his mother's mental health issues," Nikki replied softly.

Mrs. Young nodded and then continued, "A lot of us women would pitch in when she was away. Matty was good friends with my younger son, Sam. That would be Sam *senior*," she clarified as Sam Jr. delivered a tray of food to the counter. "As the years passed, he ended up spending a lot of time at our house, even when his mother was home. She was... unpredictable. I think our brand of big family chaos was easier to handle.

"That poor woman. She was such a beauty when she was young. Such spirit. And she loved Matty to the moon and back. His sister, too. And his daddy. That man was devoted to her. It was one doctor, one institution after another. Always trying to keep hope alive for his kids. This time will work. This time, Mommy will get better." There were tears in Judy's eyes; she blinked them away.

"She saw things," Judy continued. "You know that?"

Nikki nodded.

"Saw the most horrific things... her children dead on the carpet... the nightmares that any mother has, but to her they were real, and they were almost constant."

"I can't even imagine," Nikki said.

"Tragic. She tried so hard. Submitted herself to electroshock, took whatever new pills they would give her...

some just about made her comatose. Others didn't do a damned thing. Nothing worked for long. Sooner or later — and usually sooner — she'd be gone again. So I filled in where I could, that's all," Judy finished quietly.

"I'm glad you were there for him," Nikki told her, forcing the words past the ache in her throat. "He adores you."

"He's a good boy," Judy said. She blinked hard, swiping at her misty eyes, and then cleared her throat. "Go on, take him his soup."

Nikki picked up their tray and carried it to one of the long wooden tables. She waved Beth over and felt a sinking sensation as she saw her daughter surreptitiously brush a tear from her cheek.

Oh no.

When she'd left, they'd been laughing...

Nikki shot a glance at Mateo, who gave her a reassuring smile as he and Beth walked up to the table.

"That smells amazing!" Beth said. Despite the slightly bloodshot eyes, her daughter seemed more calm and settled than she had since she'd arrived in Bluebird Bay. Clearly, Nikki and Judy hadn't been the only ones having a heart to heart.

"Fresh local sourdough," Nikki told her.

"And the best clam chowder you've ever had," Mateo said.

"Obviously, you've never had my mom's clam chowder," Beth told him.

"Actually," Nikki said through a mouthful of soup, "I'm not even gonna lie. Judy's is better."

"Not possible!" Beth exclaimed, grabbing a spoon.

"She must spend a small fortune on local butter."

"Worth every penny," Mateo said.

"And she grows her own thyme."

"You're right," Beth admitted, astounded as she swallowed her first bite. "This is at least as good as yours."

They ate in silence for a while, savoring the clam chowder. It wasn't gravy-thick like restaurant chowders tended to be, but it was rich and hearty, fragrant with garlic and thyme. Nikki used her bread to sop up every last drop of the broth.

"One more game?" Beth asked as she pushed her bowl away.

"Let's do it," Nikki replied.

They bowled to the sound of sixties music, Beth surpassing Nikki's meager score after Mateo's guidance. Down at the end, a group of college-aged girls were having a blast. Nikki wondered if their presence made Beth warm to the place even more, because she had completely dropped her "emo" attitude and even the stiff awkwardness she'd walked in with.

"This place is awesome," Beth said. "So is Mrs. Young. Coolest granny ever."

"No arguments here," he agreed.

"She really is a gem," Nikki murmured in his ear, "and so are you. Thank you."

Beth was facing away from them, approaching the lane, as Nikki placed a soft, lingering kiss just to the right of his mouth.

She pulled away as Beth crowed in victory as she got her third strike of the night.

They talked and laughed as they finished a leisurely second game. When they were done, had returned their bowling shoes, and said goodbye to Mrs. Young, Mateo walked them to their car.

"It was great to meet you, Beth," Mateo said with genuine warmth. "If you ever want to talk again, feel free to reach out."

"Thanks," Beth said with a quick nod.

Mateo gave Nikki a hug and kissed her forehead. "Talk soon?"

She nodded. "Definitely."

They climbed into the car and pulled away. Nikki smiled inwardly as Beth turned and waved to Mateo one last time.

"So?" Nikki asked Beth as they pulled onto the road. "What did you think?"

"Almost definitely not a serial killer," Beth said approvingly.

"Gee, thanks."

"I like him, Mom. He seems... solid."

"I like him, too," Nikki said softly. She waited a few minutes to see if her daughter would mention the conversation she had with Mateo, but Beth just stared out the window.

"That soup was amazing," Beth said after a while. "Both of them. I wonder if she'd give up the recipes."

"I doubt she even follows one," Nikki replied. "A place like that, I think it comes down to the quality of the ingredients, and the love she puts into it. I'm convinced cooking like that is partly magic."

"I wonder if Rae would want to go bowling when I get back to school," Beth said, and Nikki smiled. If she was already talking about taking her roommate bowling, their night had definitely been a hit.

"Can't hurt to ask," Nikki said with a shrug. *And on that note...* "Hey, so what would you think of spending some time with Anna and me the day before Thanksgiving? I'm on pie duty, and our little kitchen isn't gonna cut it so she suggested we prep our dishes for the big day together at her place. I'd love it if you came."

"That sounds...not terrible, I guess," Beth said with a nod.

Nikki glanced at her daughter's beautiful face, dimly lit by street lights as they drove, and thought back to the countless pies they'd baked together over the course of her childhood.

Not terrible at all.

Now, if Thanksgiving could be even half as good...

16

TODD

"WHAT A DAY," Todd sighed as he let the door swing shut. He'd held it open for Mrs. Balaskas as she made her way through with two cat carriers. She was in the process of taming four feral kittens, and had finally managed to bring them all in for a check-up. They were nearly grown at this point, but no matter. They were fighting fit, he thought ruefully as he touched a freshly bandaged scratch on his arm.

"I've scheduled a proper lunch break for today," Nadine told him. "Doctor's orders."

"Dr. Ketterman the First, you mean?" His mother had handed the running of the clinic over to him, but she wasn't above issuing orders to Nadine here and there if she felt it necessary.

"The very same," Nadine confirmed.

"But it's our last day before we close for the holiday," Todd protested. He and his mother had planned to close for most of the week of Thanksgiving in order to get a new floor installed in the waiting room; the linoleum was roughly the same age as Todd, and he wanted to replace it with something sturdier. He was very much looking forward to the break.

"We've been so busy all day," he said. "How did you manage a lunch break?"

"By keeping you busy this morning!" Nadine said cheerfully as she walked towards the door. "You handled it beautifully. Now, go sit down somewhere and have a real meal. Your next client won't be in until one thirty."

Todd checked his watch as the door swung shut behind Nadine. That gave him two whole hours. What would he do with such a luxurious stretch of time? Without even making a conscious decision, he pulled out his phone and tapped Alice's name. She answered immediately.

"Todd, hey! Shouldn't you be removing cat ovaries or something?"

"I have an actual lunch break today," he replied. "The Great Nadine-y set me free until half past one. You're probably knee deep in dust and bird poop, but do you want to take a break for lunch? We could even stop by that jeweler after to have the ring appraised."

"I'm taking a break from Auntie's house and all that stuff today. I checked in on Barnaby this morning, but then I just went home to work on this long article I need to finish tomorrow. I was actually about to leave for lunch myself, but I promised Auntie Louise that I would have lunch with her."

"Oh, that should be nice," Todd said, trying not to let the disappointment he felt into his voice.

"It's an early Thanksgiving meal. The place where she's staying has an annual Turkey and Bingo Extravaganza on actual Thanksgiving, so she's going to go to that with her friends. I wanted to bring her those letters, and this old journal I found."

"She's lucky to have you," Todd said. "Hey, if she likes Thanksgiving food, here's a hot tip for you. There's this special happening at the deli down the street from me, an Everything But the Plate turkey sandwich. Cranberry sauce, stuffing, the whole schtick. I don't know about you, but I can never get enough Thanksgiving food. It might be my favorite holiday."

"Mine too," Alice said warmly. "Would... would you like to come with me?"

He opened his mouth and then snapped it shut.

Woah, dude. Slow down. Meeting her family already? You've been on one date with this girl.

Why did the voice in his head sound like his most annoying roommate from college?

Then again, that made it all the easier to ignore.

"I'd love to," Todd replied.

"Great!"

"I'll pick up three sandwiches and then come get you?"

"Sure, thank you."

Todd rushed out of the office and ordered three Everything But the Plates from his favorite lunch spot, then jumped into his Jeep and drove to the rental where Alice was staying. She was sitting on the front steps, wearing red corduroy pants and her purple sweater.

"I hope I didn't keep you waiting too long," Todd said.

"No, I just came outside because my roommates are screaming at each other again," Alice said, wrinkling her nose. "I might have to find a cafe to work in, or a library. Turn left up ahead."

"The library has a great area to work in. They completely redid it when I was in high school. Have you been there yet?"

"I have not, which shows more than anything how busy I've been! Between that place and writing, and Barnaby and Auntie..." Alice sighed, and then added brightly, "Bowling was fun, though!"

"With Sandy?"

"Yes with Sandy. And her friends. She's so nice, and her friends are really cool."

"How's the target training going?"

"I let him out of his cage yesterday."

"No way!"

"Yes way. He was on his best behavior, very gentlemanly. One of the nurses helped me FaceTime with Auntie Louise, and he really perked up a lot. Auntie was so happy to see him, and I didn't want her to see him locked up. So I opened the door and he climbed out, then sort of flapped over to the back of one of the chairs. You're turning right at the next light," she added quickly, and Todd changed lanes.

"When it was time for me to leave," Alice continued, "I used the target stick to lure him back to his cage. He knows now that following the stick gets him fresh fruit and his favorite nuts, so he went right back in and I loaded him up with treats."

"You missed your calling," Todd said. "It's not too late. You could join the circus, be a lion tamer."

"I didn't do much at all," Alice protested. "There, it's that building on the right."

"You moved mountains and tamed a Stymphalian!"

Alice laughed, and suddenly Todd felt overly warm in his wool sweater.

"Mountains of newspaper, yes. But Barnaby was already tame. He was just upset about Auntie. You know she's had him for longer than I've been alive?"

"Still," he said more seriously, "gaining the trust of a bird that's so bonded to his owner is no small task."

"No, it wasn't. But he was so well behaved. I'm going to try letting him out every day."

"I'm glad," Todd said as they walked up the front walk of the assisted living facility. "I think that getting out of that cage will do him a lot of good. I haven't seen Jeff, but when I do, I'll ask him about building Barnaby a nice stand."

He paused to open the door for Alice, and then continued, "We want to give him a comfortable place to hang out and climb around so that he's not pooping all over the house."

"Yes please," Alice said emphatically.

"One of the books I was looking through had a section about potty training parrots. Would you like to borrow it?"

"Definitely." Alice led him down a long hallway and knocked on one of the doors.

"Who's that?" called a surprisingly spritely voice.

"It's me, Auntie!"

"Come in, come in!"

The room was nice. Aside from the electronic hospital bed, it didn't feel too much like a hospital. There was a vase of fresh flowers, a large window, and a TV blasting a Jeopardy re-run that Aunt Louise immediately muted. She must have been eighty, but she looked bright-eyed and strong. Her white hair was cut short, and she wore a flower-patterned house dress under a button-up sweater.

"I see you found Mr. Bonomo's flower shop," Todd said

under his breath, and Alice flashed him a smile before walking towards her aunt.

"I brought a guest."

"Who's this, then?"

"Auntie, this is Dr. Todd Ketterman. He's the veterinarian who's been helping me with Barnaby."

"My nephew the doctor!" Louise greeted him.

"*Auntie!*" Alice protested, cheeks turning a delightful shade of red.

"I kid, I kid," said Louise with a chuckle. "I'd get up to greet you, but I'm afraid my old hip just isn't up to it. My physical therapist has to use a cat o' nine tails to get me out of this bed."

Alice laughed her musical laugh. "She does not, Auntie."

"It's lovely to meet you," Todd said to Louise. He held up the bag in his hand. "We brought lunch."

"He's gorgeous," said Louise in a stage whisper as Todd turned away to unpack their lunch. "If you don't nail him down, I will."

"Auntie, hush," Alice protested, still giggling.

"Sorry, sorry. Lock an old lady alone in a room with nothing but Jeopardy for company and she goes a little whackadoo. I'm delighted to see you, both of you. Thank you so much for everything you're doing for Barnaby, and for me."

"You're very welcome," Todd said. "He's a character, that bird."

"He certainly is," Louise laughed. "I've had Barnaby since he could sit in the palm of my hand. Even when he grew to be a giant, I would take him with me everywhere. I swear, he doubled attendance to the church rummage sales. People would line up for pictures."

"Oh!" Alice said suddenly. "I forgot something in the car. I'll be right back."

"Grab that pitcher for me," Louise said to Todd as Alice hurried out. "Pour me some water, and some for the two of you. There are extra cups just there."

Todd handed her a glass of water and she drank greedily. He poured two more glasses and put the pitcher where Louise could reach it.

"Thank you, dear. The nurses here are darling, but they're terribly overworked. I feel awful ringing for one each time I need a drink of water. I prefer to wait. Now, tell me. What are your intentions with my niece?"

"Sorry?" Todd mumbled.

"It's not every day that a veterinarian makes a house call to a place where the pet is *not*. So, either my Barnaby is dying and you're here to break the news to me gently, or you like my Alice quite a lot. And, as I fully expect that bird to outlive me, I'm guessing it's the latter."

"Barnaby is in pretty good health."

"Ah *ha*!" Louise said, and then chuckled. "Look at you blush. All right, I won't pry. At least, not on that subject. But quick, before she comes back. Tell me how Alice is holding up." The older woman's face grew serious. "She showed me some pictures of the living room. This may sound crazy, but I had forgotten how big it was. Things accumulated so slowly, over time... I saw those pictures and realized that I was just like a frog in a pot. It happened so gradually that I didn't realize I was being boiled alive. I got a lecture from my brother — my *younger* brother, mind you — about how hard Alice was working, clearing all that old junk out of there."

"Alice is holding up just fine," Todd assured her. "She's strong."

"This place is neat as a pin," Louise murmured, looking around her room. "I'd forgotten what that felt like. It was so foreign, at first, having all this space around me. I'll confess, it gave me a touch of the vertigo. But I do believe I'm getting used to it. And to having people around, too. There she is!" Louise exclaimed as Alice came back in.

"You're not eating yet?" Alice asked.

"We were waiting for you. What's that you're holding?"

"It's a surprise," Alice said, setting it on a table and picking up a box of food. "Let's eat first. Here, it's the deli's special Thanksgiving sandwich."

"What a delightful mess," Louise said as she opened her box. "I do believe I'll need a fork."

Alice fetched her one, and they enjoyed their food in relative silence. Occasionally, Louise would blurt out a non-sequitur, and Todd would look over to see that she was giving the answer to the current Jeopardy question.

"That was delicious," Louise said at last, "but it will last me at least another two meals." She set the box aside. "Now, where's my surprise?"

Alice set aside her own oversized sandwich and washed her hands, then picked up the bundle she had fetched.

"I found some letters, Auntie, and an old journal. We didn't read anything, but it looks like the letters were from Uncle Ernie?"

"No!" Louise gasped, reaching for the letters. "I thought I'd lost those years ago! I was certain they were the victim of one of my recycling drives." Her eyes misted over as she saw the handwriting on the yellowed pages. "Oh, Ernest," she said softly. "He sent me these from Vietnam. You know he wasn't even drafted?" She glanced up at Alice and back down to the letters. "He volunteered. One of the first. Patriotic fool," she murmured fondly.

"There's this, too." Alice handed her the journal.

"Oh," Louise murmured, stroking the cover. "I wrote this when I was just a girl. I was thrifty, made it last nearly ten years." She looked up at Alice. "I lived in an orphanage on and off, you know."

Alice's eyes went soft. "I know, Auntie."

"I wrote most of this when I was living with the nuns. I didn't have anyone else to talk to, most days."

"Nuns?" Alice asked. "I don't think I knew that part."

"That's where the orphans went. We lived in town," Louise said slowly, paging through the old journal. "Flour sack dresses, never enough to eat... Daddy didn't own the house, and eventually we had no choice but to move in with his folks. His mother was a hard woman. Times were so tough. They couldn't feed so many mouths, so Daddy left, looking for work. After a couple of years, Gram said that I had to go, too. It was me or my brother, and I was older. Mama would have gone — she hardly ate a thing, herself — but she knew that there was a good chance Gram would starve the both of us if she left. So she found a place for me at a convent."

"They kept me fed," she continued. "There was always enough to eat, if only just. Fresh produce, even. There was an orchard at the convent, and a wonderful garden. They let me give my family peaches sometimes, or tomatoes. The place was about two hours away from my grandparents' house, walking. My mother would come every weekend to visit me, her and Billy both. During the week I scrubbed floors, collected eggs, weeded the garden... it wasn't so bad. This journal was the only thing I owned, not counting my two dresses. I had to beg the sisters to let me borrow their pens. They were kindly, most of them. I lived there for four years," she finished softly.

"Do you think that's why you've held on to everything?" Alice suggested gently. Glossy black curls bounced alongside her face as she leaned towards her aunt.

Louise looked up at her in surprise. "What do you mean?"

"Well, you had so little growing up. I could see how that might make it hard to let go of the things that you have now."

"I never cared about *things*," Louise said crossly. "I never had trouble letting go of things. I saved up newspapers and cans so that I could recycle them properly, that's all. I ran the town's recycling program for fifteen years before the government stepped up and took over. And I always donated a carload of things to the church rummage sale every year."

"I know you did, Auntie."

"So!" Louise said with emphasis. "I don't care about things. I just... it's such a dreadful waste to throw things away when there are people out there who have nothing at all. As I grew older, it became harder to bring things to their proper places. I handed the church rummage sale to Patty White and that woman ran it for all of two years before she canceled it altogether. I was not attached to those piles of newspapers, young miss. I was waiting for the opportunity to dispose of them properly."

"I understand, Auntie. The newspapers all got recycled, and I took most of your old clothes to the women's shelter."

Louise's expression softened. "You're a gem, Alice. Thank you."

"That reminds me!" Alice said brightly. "One last surprise."

She pulled the old aspirin bottle from her pocket and handed it to Louise.

"You're too kind," said the old lady.

"Open it," Alice laughed.

"Oh my lord," Louise said reverently as the ring fell into her palm. "Another piece of my history that I thought was gone forever."

"Did Uncle Ernie give it to you?"

"God, no," Louise cackled. "It was an old suitor who tried to steal me away from Ernie while he was off in Vietnam. Of all the low-down dirty tricks..."

"And you kept it?" Alice said with a laugh. Todd realized that he was staring at her, that he had been even while Aunt Louise was speaking. He didn't try to stop himself. What sort of man looked away from a sunrise?

"He insisted, and I didn't argue."

The alarm on Todd's phone went off, and he winced, hating to cut this short. Auntie Louise was a treasure.

"You gotta go, Doctor?" she asked with a smile.

"I'm so sorry, ladies, but I do need to be getting back to work."

"You kids get out of here," Louise said. "I won't keep you."

"It was lovely to finally meet you, Louise." Todd gave her hand a light squeeze. "You take care, and listen to that physical therapist. Barnaby misses you."

"It was lovely meeting you, Dr. Ketterman. You take care."

As Todd turned to go, he heard her whisper to Alice, "That one is a *keeper*."

Alice's cheeks were rosy as she joined him in the hall.

"Come to Thanksgiving with me," Todd said impetuously. "If you aren't going back home?"

Alice looked up at him with wide eyes.

"On Thursday," he continued stupidly, as if she didn't know when Thanksgiving was. "You could come to my mother's house for Thanksgiving dinner. She and her sisters always cook enough food to feed an army. My little brother will be there, and we can talk to him about building that stand for Barnaby. My cousin Max will be there, too, and you can talk about—"

Alice interrupted him with a kiss and then pulled away.

"I'd like that," she said with a smile. "I'd like that a lot."

17

ANNA

"It smells wonderful in here!" Beckett said as he walked into the kitchen. "What's cooking?"

"I'm just toasting some glazed pecans for the salad," Anna said, peeking into the oven. Not quite done. "That's what my sisters trust me to bring for Thanksgiving. A salad."

"You make a mean salad," Beckett told her. "And seriously, your lasagna is untouchable. But I heard about that one time you were tasked with making the turkey..."

"Oh my God, they tell everyone that story. Is nothing sacred anymore?" she said with a grumble. "I swear, you'd think I was the first person to ever cook a bird with the plastic bag of giblets still inside it."

She went to get herself a glass of water and fumbled, dropping the glass. It rolled off of the counter, and Beckett caught it before it crashed to the floor. He filled it with water and handed it to her with exaggerated care.

"Nervous?" he asked mildly.

She eyed him dubiously. "Is it just me, or is a sullen

teenager in a crowded kitchen a recipe for disaster? Hide the steak knives."

Beckett chuckled and moved behind her to rub her shoulders.

"It's great that she agreed to come over," he said.

"Her mom probably almost forced her at gunpoint." Then, Anna remembered that Nikki had *actually* been held at gunpoint a month before, and her weak joke made her stomach roil.

They weren't even here yet, and she was already saying the wrong thing. What if she made an already tough situation even worse?

"I don't know how to do this," she groaned.

"You have two nieces and three nephews who already adore you," Beckett said as he dug his thumbs in around her shoulder blades. Anna groaned again, this time in pleasure.

"Yeah, but I got in early. It's easy to be the cool aunt when they're little. Do you know how easy it is to impress a kindergartener? All I had to do was let them eat ice cream before dinner and let them play dress up in my closet. But a teenager that I don't even know? How am I supposed to impress her?"

"You don't have to impress her," Beckett chuckled. "Just talk to her. Be yourself."

She arched a brow at him. "Are you saying that I'm not impressive when I'm being myself?"

"You are very impressive. Anna Sullivan, jet-setting Wonder Woman, world-renowned wildlife photographer, maker of excellent salads. You impress me daily."

Anna laughed and then stopped short as she heard a

knock on the door. Beckett had done a great job distracting her from the clock, she realized with a start.

She crossed the room and opened the door to find the front stoop crowded with familiar faces.

"Look who we met when we pulled in!" Austin said with a grin. Beckett's son was struggling to keep a good grip on Teddy, who was attempting to launch himself into Beth's arms.

"Bear!" he shouted, reaching for the knit cap that Beth wore with a teddy bear face emblazoned on it.

Nikki was juggling multiple bags of groceries and Anna grabbed one.

"Come on in out of the cold, gang," she said as she led them into the house.

"Bear!" Teddy repeated, still angling to get to Beth.

"I...I can hold him if you'd like," Beth murmured.

By the time everyone was inside and had taken their coats off, Teddy had the bear hat, and Beth had Teddy.

"He just woke up from a good long nap," Austin told Beckett, handing over Teddy's diaper bag. "Hopefully, the dentist won't take more than an hour or so, and then I'm going to stop by the grocery store. The cupboards are bare," he growled playfully, looking at his son.

"Bear!" Teddy crowed. "My bear!"

"I'll be back before three," Austin said.

"No rush," Beckett told him. "We kind of like this guy." Austin waved goodbye to Teddy and headed out. Nikki was emptying grocery bags and sorting ingredients.

"I brought everything but the salt, I think. We've got pumpkin, pecan, blueberry, and apple."

"What a feast!" Beckett said.

"It's a big family," Nikki said shyly. "I wasn't sure what everyone's favorites were, or I would've made doubles. I did bring an extra-large pie tin for the pumpkin."

"Good call," Anna approved. "A paltry nine-inch pumpkin pie will not satisfy the Sullivan clan."

"Teddy down!" a small voice insisted. Beth set him free, and he immediately grabbed her hand to pull her down the hall. "Dawk noom!"

Beth gave Anna a bewildered glance over one shoulder, and Anna laughed.

"He loves the dark room. Here, I'll unlock the door." She slipped ahead of them and opened the unnecessarily complicated baby lock they'd installed to keep Teddy from getting into the chemicals she used to process her photos.

"Dese aw Nana's wooks in pwogwess," he informed Beth solemnly. "Awt takes time."

"Art does take time, Teddy. Thanks for showing me," Beth crooned in a melted-butter voice. She was in love already, and Anna couldn't blame her. Teddy was the perfect ice breaker. She should pop him into a hiking backpack and take him with her everywhere she went to soften her rough edges and bring the charm.

"Come see my toys!" Teddy demanded, pulling her across the hall to his bedroom. "Wook! My bear!" He grabbed the stuffed animal from his bed and shoved Beth's hat over its ears. He looked back up at Beth. "You weed me books?" he asked.

"I would love to read you books." Beth grabbed a stack of board books and sat with her back to the bed. Anna decided to give her some space to settle in. She didn't want to unnerve the girl by hovering.

"We'll be in the kitchen if you need anything."

"Thanks...Aunt Anna," Beth said. The look on her face said she was trying the name on for size, and Anna's heart warmed. She was a good kid in a very confusing situation and she was handling it all pretty darned well, in Anna's opinion.

By the time she returned to the kitchen, Nikki was rolling out the pie crusts.

"You work *fast*," Anna said, and Nikki laughed.

"We made the dough last night. I like to let it chill for at least twelve hours."

Anna pulled out a cutting board and started on the apples.

"How are things going with you two?" she asked.

"Better," Nikki replied. "It was dicey for a while there — she tried to burrow into the couch at our rental — but last night I got her to go to Young's Bowling Alley."

"Oh, I love that place!" Anna said.

"Me too. And Mateo *really* does, it's like a second home to him. He met us there."

"Beth met Mateo? How did *that* go?"

"It went really well. I don't know what he said to her, but she really came out of her shell. Judy's clam chowder didn't hurt."

"It never does," Anna said agreeably. "I'm glad you both came today."

Nikki met her sister's eyes. "Me too."

"Boobies!" Teddy shouted from down the hall, and Nikki snickered.

"Is he, uh, hungry, or?"

"He is, but not for *that*," Anna said. "His mom weaned him a long time ago."

176

Teddy appeared, still dragging Beth by the hand.

"Boobies!" he demanded.

Beth looked at her aunt with wide eyes, obviously trying not to laugh.

"We do have blueberries, Teddy." Anna grabbed one of his plastic bowls and filled it with some of the blueberries Nikki had brought for pie filling. Then, she hefted him into his high chair.

She went back to chopping apples as Teddy made a gleeful mess of his berries.

"Can I help?" Beth asked.

"Of course!" Nikki said. "I was thinking we'd bake the pumpkin and fruit pies first. The pumpkin will need its own rack. Do you want to make the filling?"

"I'm on it."

"Great. All the spices are right there."

"Where's your stand mixer, Aunt Anna?"

Anna laughed. "I'm not a chef. You'll have to mix it up the old fashioned way."

"By hand?" Beth asked incredulously.

"Build them muscles!"

Beth laughed and picked up a whisk.

"Teddy down!" insisted the sticky creature that some mischievous fairy had swapped for Beckett's grandson. "I hep!"

"Okay, Teddy. Come help." Anna lifted him onto her hip and carried him over to the counter. "Want to help me mix the sugar and cinnamon with the apple slices?"

"I hep!" Teddy said happily, shoving an apple slice into his mouth.

Anna scooped up some sugar with one hand and gave the measuring cup to Teddy.

"Here, bud, put this on the apples."

Teddy tried to pour the sugar straight into his mouth like a drink, and Anna shrieked with laughter as she intercepted him. "Into the *bowl*, you little sugar monster!"

The boy laughed and curled his hands into claws. "Suga monsta!" he declared, and bared his teeth in a snarl.

Beckett walked in and laughed at the sight of his sugar-crusted grandson.

"I'm guessing things would go a bit faster *without* the sugar monster?" he said.

"I da suga monsta!" Teddy said delightedly, trying to wrest the cup of sugar out of Anna's hands.

"Hmm... does anyone know where Teddy went? I need him to help me drive the tow truck."

Teddy immediately released the cup and raised two purple hands to his grandfather.

"I Teddy! I me, Grampa!"

"Oh *there* you are!" Beckett said, scooping him up and throwing him over one shoulder. Teddy shrieked with laughter as Beckett carried him out of the kitchen.

"I think I just got dumped for a tow truck," Anna said.

"That's okay, he dumped me for boobies," Beth said, and all three of them laughed.

Delicious smells filled the kitchen as Anna roasted a second batch of pecans for pie and Nikki set blueberry pie filling to bubble on the stove.

"Those berries smell like summertime," Anna said with a sigh. "My mom would make blueberry pie all summer long. Her cousin owned a farm about an hour south of here, and we would go at least a couple times a month and pick berries all day long. She'd freeze a few, can a few, and of course we'd eat as many as we could fit in our greedy little bellies. But mostly she would make the most delicious pies."

"We used to go berry picking in the summertime, too. But we'd mostly go hunting for wild berries. Dad loved camping, and my mom hated it. But she would always agree to go if it meant a day of collecting wild blueberries."

"I miss her," Anna said softly. "My mom. I can't believe she's been gone as long as she has."

"I miss mine, too," Nikki said. Identical hazel eyes met across the kitchen, and they shared a sorrowful smile.

Beth muttered something unintelligible and rushed out, one hand shielding her face.

"I should go talk to her," Nikki said, turning off the stove.

"Can I try?" Anna asked on impulse. Nikki looked to her in surprise.

"Sure."

"Keep cooking, chef. We'll be back in a jiff."

Anna found Beth sitting on the porch swing, sniffling. She sat down beside her, tucking her hands into her armpits against the chill of the evening air.

"Still upset that Teddy dumped you?" she teased gently.

Beth shrugged, looking the other way.

"Just overwhelmed?" Anna asked.

"Yeah," Beth said in a voice choked with tears. "I don't know what's wrong with me. Everyone in Bluebird Bay has been super nice. My mom's happier than I've seen her since... maybe ever. And then I came and ruined it all."

"You didn't ruin anything," Anna told her.

"I did. She's worried about me. I'm stressing her out. I

don't want to, I just... don't know how to stop. I'm all over the place. One minute, I feel like I hate her for skipping town without telling me. The next moment, I just want her to hold me like she did when I was a little kid. Like just now."

"It's complicated stuff," Anna said softly, "mothers and daughters."

"When you guys were talking about your moms, I was thinking about my grandma," Beth said. "She was the sweetest. I don't think I ever even saw her mad. We all used to make pies together all the time, her and my mom and me. And then I thought about my grandpa cheating on her and I was just so pissed off. But it's freaking impossible to be angry at Grandpa for long, you know? He's the nicest guy on the planet."

"No," Anna said quietly. "I don't know."

"Oh. Right. Sorry." Beth shot her a quick, quizzical look. "I never knew my dad, either. But if it turned out he was a good guy, or even just a normal guy... I would have wanted to. Get to know him, I mean. Don't you want to meet Grandpa Eric? Aren't you curious? You look like him, you know."

Anna winced. "The thing is, I *had* a dad. A great one."

"And you have another great one who is still alive. That's two to my zero. Is that so bad?"

Anna took a long, deep breath, the words landing like a body blow. On paper, it looked so simple.

"What's he like, this grandpa of yours?"

"Oh, he's just the nicest guy on the planet. After we moved to Cherry Blossom Point, I didn't even miss having a dad. Grandpa was way better than any of my friends' dads. He never yelled at me or, like, checked out and ignored me. He was always there. Any school stuff that a dad was supposed to go to, Grandpa Eric was there for me." There were tears in her eyes again. "How could he be such an amazing grandpa and such a crappy husband?"

"People are complicated," Anna told her niece, and she found herself reluctantly defending the father she had never met. "He made a mistake. That doesn't mean he was a totally bad husband."

Hell, he gave up a daughter to appease his wife. He must have loved her somewhat.

"I guess. They always *seemed* happy together."

"It's okay to love people who have made mistakes. We all do. You know, kiddo, if you can extend that compassion you have for your grandparents to all of the people in your life, you're going to be an amazing woman."

Beth released a little *hmph* of laughter through her tears.

"I'm not a hundred percent sure I've gotten all the brat out of me yet," she told her aunt. "It's a work in progress."

"Same here, kiddo. And there's nothing wrong with that. Anything worth doing takes time."

"Thanks, Aunt Anna," Beth said, standing. "We should go back in and help my mom. Also, I'm freezing."

"Come here."

Anna stood and pulled an unresisting Beth in for a quick hug that the girl returned without hesitation.

Anna had never been a big hugger, but with family, she gave in to the urge sometimes. She was surprised to find that it felt normal with Beth. Easy. No different from hugging Max or Sarah.

She waited for the instinctive denial to come. The thoughts that had plagued her for so long after she found out about her biological father and the Merrills, about real family, but they never came.

As she pulled away and followed her curly-haired niece back inside, she realized she was truly past that now.

Nikki and Beth were family. No qualifiers, no "half" this, or "sort of" that.

Just family.

And it felt good.

18

CEE-CEE

Cᴇᴇ-ᴄᴇᴇ ᴘᴜᴛ the finishing touches on her contribution to the Sullivan family Thanksgiving feast and stood back with a happy sigh. Steph's house smelled divine and she breathed in deeply. The scent of sausage and sage stuffing, roasting turkey, and yeasty rolls baking in the oven made her mouth water. And she was majorly proud of what she'd brought over.

Ever since she had opened her shop, cupcakes had become everyday fare for the whole family. When she'd told her sisters she wanted to do something different, Anna had jokingly challenged her to make turkey-and-stuffing cupcakes. Taking to the idea, Cee-cee had risen to the occasion. She had made miniature meatloaves with a mixture of turkey and pork, infused with sage gravy. She'd covered them with sourdough crust, and had just finished slathering mashed potatoes and cranberry sauce over the top each.

"Seriously, they look just like cupcakes!" Steph marveled as she bustled by with an empty tray.

The kitchen was bustling as Steph, Nikki, and Anna

finished heating or prepping their own dishes, but Cee-cee was already dreaming up the next phase of her business. People already stopped by the shop for breakfast and lunch. What if they offered savory muffins every day for people who needed something more solid before their sugar fix? She could make quiches in her muffin tins, hamburger-themed individual meatloaves, hearty muffins with ham and cheese... there could be a whole display case for savory options, and—

She stopped short, pulling her mind back into the present. It was a good idea, but business could wait. Today was about family.

"That's it for the meat-cakes," she said to Steph. "Need a hand with anything?"

"I think we're just about done," her sister said happily. She pulled some heat resistant pads out of a drawer and handed them to Cee-cee.

"Would you put these on the dining table, please? All the veggies are just about ready to go out."

Cee-cee accepted the pads and went into the dining room, where Jeff and Beth were setting the table. She laid them down in strategic positions as she listened to them chatter about some game. It was all Greek to her, but she was pleased to hear how easily the two kids had hit it off.

"That is super weird," Beth said gleefully as she arranged the silverware. "I love it. Have you seen the teddy bear on the empty chairs?"

"No," Jeff said with a laugh, almost losing his grip on the precarious stack of glasses that he held. "I *have* seen the giant dinosaur footprint."

"The one that flattened the house? That was a nice touch."

Ethan came up the stairs from the basement carrying an armload of folding chairs, followed by Mick. With both extra leaves in, the dining table should accommodate the whole crowd...

Sarah and her husband Oliver were spending the holiday with his family. They would join the Sullivans for Christmas. Stephanie would have to get used to sharing; that was the mixed blessing of kids getting married.

Cee-cee had no holiday competition from in-laws, she realized with a guilty start. Sasha was an orphan, which meant that Cee-cee would always have her son and granddaughter home for the holidays. Max's boyfriend Ian didn't get along with his parents, so they would likely show up for most holidays with the Sullivans, as well. She wouldn't look a gift horse in the mouth, but she did feel sad for both of them. She'd just make an extra effort to ensure they felt included, like family.

This would mark their first holiday season without Pop, and Eva had begged off, opting to head to her cousin's house in Sanford. Cee-cee wondered if she wasn't quite ready for a big, boisterous Sullivan holiday without him. Steph's husband Paul's absence would always be felt, as would their mother's, but the empty seats were filled and then some. Nikki and Beth were here, and Todd had brought a date at the last minute, a stunning young woman who was fairly new to Bluebird Bay.

Cee-cee scanned the place settings, doing a final headcount. Yes, they would all fit. If only just.

"What's the score, Beckett?" Mick called into the living room.

"You're still down by one!" Anna's boyfriend shouted.

"Go," Cee-cee said with a laugh. "We'll finish up."

Mick grinned at her. "Fine, but I'm doing the dishes."

"No arguments here." She gave him a kiss on the cheek and a gentle shove towards the door. She had just finished arranging the chairs when she heard Gabe and Sasha at the front door. Cee-cee rushed out to greet them. Sasha's belly looked twice as big as the last time that Cee-cee had seen her.

"Oh, our little Gracie is growing so fast," she crooned as she greeted them with hugs. She extended a hand towards Sasha's belly. "May I?"

"Sure." Sasha's face was flushed from the chill wind that blew outside. She looked bright-eyed and happy, with a healthy roundness to her cheeks. For the first half of the pregnancy, she had been so wan and thin. But she and Gabe had rebuilt their relationship after a rocky start to their marriage, and now she was glowing.

Cee-cee rested her hand on Sasha's belly.

"Is she busy in there today?" she asked her daughter-in-law.

"So busy!" Sasha replied, paying her hand over Cee-cee's and moving it a little lower, to the right.

Suddenly, there was a light *thump* against Cee-cee's palm. A knee, or maybe an elbow, moved beneath her hand, and tears filled Cee-cee's eyes.

"I already love her so much," she said to Sasha.

"Me too," Sasha said with feeling.

"Me three," Gabe chimed in. He had an arm slung around Sasha's shoulders, but his eyes were already on the game. All of the men plus Todd's date, Alice, shouted at the screen as someone scored or fumbled or whatever it was they did.

"Go on." Sasha gave him a playful shove. He grinned at her and joined the other men on the couch.

"Come on into the kitchen. We have hot cider on the stove," Cee-cee said, taking hold of Sasha's arm.

"Thanks, Mom," Sasha said shyly.

I hope motherhood builds her confidence, Cee-cee thought as she ushered Sasha into the kitchen, where her sisters stood sipping wine. Sasha's place in the family still felt a little fragile after the rough time she and Gabe had gone through, and Cee-cee wanted her to feel at home with them. Well, that would happen more and more with time, she reflected as she poured Sasha a mug of cider. Cee-cee would make sure to never criticize the young woman's parenting.

Just food and love and praise, Cee-cee thought as she handed Sasha her spiced apple cider. *She'll feel like a real Sullivan girl soon enough.*

"Have a bite to eat," Cee-cee told her, steering Sasha towards the platter of food that they had been snacking on as they cooked. There was brie with honey, a pile of crackers, and sliced pears topped with goat cheese and cranberry sauce.

"Hi, Mom!" Max walked into the kitchen with Ian. "Where's the wine?"

"Good to see you, too," Cee-cee laughed, hugging her daughter.

"Sorry." Max gave her a wry smile. "I spent the morning in the shop. I want to take the rest of this week off — we're closed for the holiday weekend — but there is *so* much inventory to do to prepare for the Christmas rush. Monday's going to be a beast."

"I'm sure," Cee-cee poured her daughter a glass of wine.

"But let's leave work at work. Just for today. No books. No cupcakes."

"I see cupcakes," Max teased as Cee-cee poured a glass of wine for Ian.

"Nope!" Cee-cee said cheerfully. "They're individual meatloaves."

"They're what?" Max laughed, taking a closer look. Cee-cee listed off the ingredients as her sisters began ferrying food out to the table.

"Is it that time?" she asked Stephanie as she walked past, bearing a tray of green-bean casserole in two gloved hands.

"No time like the present!" she said cheerfully.

Cee-cee grabbed her mini meatloaves.

"Round up the troops," she told her daughter. Max saluted smartly.

"Sir, yes sir!"

There was a moment of chaos as everyone shuffled for a seat at the table. Cee-cee found herself sitting across from Todd and his date. Max sat to her right with Ian on her other side, and Mick claimed the seat to her left.

"We haven't been properly introduced in all the chaos," Cee-cee said to Todd's doe-eyed girlfriend. "I'm Todd's Aunt Cee-cee."

"The matriarch of the Sullivan clan," Max interrupted with a smirk.

"This is my daughter Max and her boyfriend Ian," Cee-cee continued, "and this is Mick."

"I'm Alice." The girl flashed them a brilliant smile, white teeth bright against her dark red lipstick. Her lustrous curls were held back by a bright red headscarf, and she wore a long-sleeved red dress. The color suited her, and Cee-cee noticed that Todd couldn't keep his eyes off of her.

"I'm so grateful to be here," Alice said earnestly. "I didn't think I'd get a real Thanksgiving meal this year. I was planning on apple pie and game shows with Barnaby."

Todd laughed as Max asked, "Who is Barnaby?"

"He's a Stymphalian bird," Todd told her.

Max raised an eyebrow and said to Alice, "You're friends with a bronze-feathered man eater?"

"You are the *only* person who would get that reference," Todd crowed.

"Barnaby is a great green macaw," said Alice with another sparkling smile. "I'm taking care of him for my Aunt Louise."

"Louise Fredrickson?" Cee-cee asked.

"The very same!" Alice said brightly.

"I know her and totally see the resemblance! She used to run the church rummage sales. I haven't seen her in years. A mutual friend told me that she broke her hip?" Cee-cee added with a frown.

"She did," Alice confirmed.

"But not her spirit," Todd added, serving Alice a hearty portion of mashed potatoes.

"No, she's a firecracker," said Alice with a grin.

"Where is she staying?" Cee-cee asked.

"Do you know the place over on 5th?"

"I do! We almost put our father there. It's a lovely place. It was my first choice, if we were going to put him in a care facility. But he moved in with Steph, in the end."

"It's a great option if you can manage it."

"Though not always the easiest," Todd added.

"We can't find anyplace that will allow her to bring Barnaby, so we're trying to figure out what to do next... it isn't easy."

"No," Cee-cee agreed. "We turned our lives upside down to care for our father in his final years. Not that I would change it, but it's tough. Louise is so lucky to have a niece that would uproot her life just to come here to help. Most people wouldn't do that for their own parents."

Alice flushed, looking down as she passed along a basket of rolls.

"There wasn't much to uproot. I had just graduated and didn't really have a full-time career yet. Auntie Louise was always so kind to me... she would send things cross-country the whole time I was in school, and she was always calling to check in. She wanted to hear all of the details about my classes, the books I was reading...

"Which reminds me," she said brightly, turning toward Max. "We have boxes and boxes of books in Todd's car. There are tons of classics, gorgeous editions, maybe even some rare ones? He said you might want to have a look?"

"For sure!" Max said. "I love old books. It's why I do what I do."

"Do you sell large-print books? Auntie loves to read, but her eyes aren't what they used to be. I've tried setting her up with audiobooks, but she doesn't like them much. And she *hated* the kindle I gave her, even though you can make the words as big as you like. She wants the real thing."

"I don't have many large-print books in stock, but I could definitely find some. What does she like?"

The girls chatted about books as Cee-cee accepted the salad bowl from Mick and helped herself to a large serving.

Roasted pecans, apple slices, pomegranate seeds, herbed goat cheese, and a tangy vinaigrette. Cee-cee could hardly wait to dig in. Anna was on salad duty for life. She had also made cranberry sauce from scratch, using fresh orange juice and finely grated ginger.

She piled her plate high, taking some of everything. In addition to providing them with this year's pies, Nikki had contributed crispy brussels sprouts and a cheesy cauliflower mash. Stephanie had handled the turkey and stuffing, which both smelled amazing. What a feast this was, and what a family. She let out a sigh of contentment.

She took a bite of buttery mashed potatoes and reflected on how many Thanksgivings she had denied herself her favorites. Nate would raise an eyebrow as she reached for the gravy or a second helping of stuffing.

She was in the middle of that thought when Mick snuck another roll onto Cee-cee's plate, and she squeezed his leg under the table. She wouldn't let Nate darken the doorstep of her thoughts. Not today. She wouldn't dwell on the decades that she had spent under his thumb, or his attempts to lure her back. She wouldn't worry about his monumentally awful decisions or the effect that they might have on Max and Gabe. Today was a day to be present, enjoy the phenomenal food, and delight in the company of her extended, and extensive, family.

Beside her, Max and Alice were deep in conversation about the Bronte sisters. Towards the end of the table, Jeff and Beth were having an animated and cheerful argument about the pros and cons of online chess. It was enough to see how easily Beth was fitting in, and how much the youngest members of the family were enjoying themselves.

Not the youngest for long, she thought with a glance toward Sasha. Gabe had piled her plate high with all her favorites, and she was eating like it was her job. And it was, sort of. She was growing a baby inside her, and that took a lot of energy. Once they were past the holidays, Cee-cee would start prepping post-partum meals. There was plenty of room in the commercial freezer at the cupcake shop and not every baby waited until their due date to make an entrance.

At the far end of the table, Nikki and Anna were engaged in an animated discussion about Anna's trip to Hawaii. Her boyfriend Beckett was normally a man of few words, but he was talking now — some anecdote about their encounter with a group of wild boar. She hadn't heard that one. Well, no surprise. Anna tried to shield Cee-cee from hearing about her most hair-raising adventures. Not that wild boar held a candle to the wolves she had worked with... though maybe they did. Cee-cee revised her opinion as Beckett described the animals' huge tusks and Anna waxed eloquent about the bloodthirsty red gleam in their eyes. Cee-cee shook her head with a smile and turned her attention to her food.

The meal passed in a pleasant haze, and Cee-cee was groggy with food and turkey before the desserts even made their appearance. Still, she had to at least *try* each of the pies that Nikki had crafted with such care.

With pie and hot coffee on the brain, she stood to clear some plates, and Ian followed her into the kitchen with a stack of his own.

"Would you open another bottle of wine?" Cee-cee asked him as she began to load the dishwasher.

"Of course," he said agreeably, selecting a bottle of red table wine from the nearby rack. "This one?"

"Sure."

"Can I ask you something?" Ian's head was down as he opened the bottle, but she could hear a note of concern in his voice.

"Of course," she asked, pausing her work.

"What's wrong?" he asked gently.

Cee-cee looked at him in surprise. "What do you mean? It's been a great day."

"Yeah, but every once in a while you get pensive and look at Max. I can see that you're worried."

Cee-cee wrinkled her nose. "Is it that obvious?"

Ian shrugged. "She didn't notice," he said with a wry smile. "She wouldn't, not when there's someone to talk Bronte with. But it's got me concerned."

Cee-cee sighed and dried her hands on a dishcloth. "I wasn't going to say anything today, I don't want to ruin her holiday. But... Nate is having some financial troubles, and I'm worried about him. He's in deep, Ian. I'm trying to think of how to help, and Nate claims that he has some irons in the fire—" she broke off and waved a hand. "You know what? I'm sure it will be okay. I'm just a worrywart," she added with false cheer. "It's part of being a mom."

Ian nodded as Max walked in with an empty casserole dish.

"What's up with you?" Max asked her boyfriend, frowning. "You look like someone just ate the last slice of apple pie." She froze in place and widened her eyes comically. "Did someone just eat the last slice of apple pie?" she demanded.

"Nope. I just caught sight of all my dessert options and

am having a serious war within," he said with a grin. "Too many choices. I see sweatpants in my future."

Mick came through the door with a stack of plates.

"I'm going to need some coffee to get through these dishes." He spotted Cee-cee and exclaimed, "Hey! You! Put down that rag and step away from the dishwasher. Right. This. Minute."

Cee-cee laughed and did as he demanded. "I was just starting the first load."

"That wasn't the deal," he said sternly. "You go put your feet up."

She stood on tiptoe to kiss him over the stack of plates that he held.

"If you insist." She threw an arm around Max's shoulders and led her daughter out to the living room, asking, "Did you bring that new board game you've been talking about?"

This was a day for giving thanks, and that was exactly what Cee-cee intended to do. Just one day of fun and games, feasting and family. God, she was *so* thankful for this big, beautiful, ever-expanding family. She was so lucky to have all of these wonderful people in her life, old *and* new.

Nate's problems were for another day.

19

TODD

THE BOARD GAME Max had brought was a dizzying mix of colored tiles and tiny game pieces, all representing different types of land and settlements connected by roads. Todd studied the cards in his hand, figuring out which resources he would need to build another city.

"I'll trade you three sheep for two stone," he offered.

"Deal!" Max said with unsettling eagerness, snatching the cards from his hand. She bought a development card and slammed it down on the table in triumph. "Library! I win!"

"This game is lame."

"You're just saying that because Max won three games in a row," Ian told him.

"My turn!" Alice said with a grin.

"Yes, another game!" Max said. "Who's in?"

"Me," said Ian.

"I'll try," Stephanie volunteered with a dubious shrug.

"Anyone need another drink?" Todd asked as he stood up.

"No thanks, sweetie."

"I'm good," Max said, eyes on the game as she rearranged the board.

"I'll take some more of that cider," Alice told him. The red dress she wore was modest, but it hugged her in all the right places. It was no wonder that he couldn't pay attention to Max's complicated new game.

"Coming right up." Todd took Alice's glass into the kitchen and filled it with warm cider. He grabbed an IPA from the fridge and went back into the dining room, where games were being played at both ends of the table. Alice was absorbed in the process of setting out her first pieces, but she gave Todd a grin and a word of thanks as he set down her glass.

"Go there, Steph," Alice advised Todd's mother. "That gives you stone and wheat, and you can use that port to trade."

Bored with Settlers of Catan and not wanting to get caught staring at Alice the whole time, Todd wandered to the opposite end of the extended dining table, where Sasha and Beth were playing Connect Four. Gabe and Jeff sat next to them, eating the last of a pumpkin pie.

Todd sat at the head of the table, and Pop's face flashed through his head. He was surprised by how much he missed him. His father's absence was a wound that would always be there... still, years later, it had yet to fade into a scar that only hurt when he poked it. After his father's untimely death, he hadn't thought Pop's would hit him so hard.

"Put a disk there!" Jeff told Sasha, pointing.

"No fair!" Beth protested as Sasha blocked her. She sounded like she was enjoying herself.

Mick walked by the table, slipping Jeff a beer with a

wink. Jeff would be twenty-one in two months, and no one minded, but the covert handoff had Todd smiling to himself.

He was so grateful that Jeff had found a father figure in Mick. The age difference between the brothers wasn't wide enough for Todd to fill that role. Their mom's boyfriend Ethan was cool, but his job kept him pretty busy. Jeff had obviously needed some guidance, and Aunt Cee-cee's fiancé had stepped up. Already a warm sort of affection was growing between the carpenter and his apprentice.

There was laughter from the other end of the table, and Todd chanced a glance at Alice. She was teasing Max, encouraging Stephanie to build a road that would cut her niece off from the port she was headed for. Her laughter lit up the room.

I'm going to miss that laugh.

The thought hit him like a punch to the stomach.

He was falling for her. No use denying it. How had this happened? All of his adult life and then some, he had pursued veterinary school with laser-focus. He'd had a girlfriend through most of his years at Cornell, but they were both in vet school and busy as hell. It had been pleasant to have the companionship through long hours of studying, but that had been it. When he and Chelsea had moved to different states to pursue their careers after graduation, they had broken up with no hard feelings.

After *years*.

Todd hadn't even known Alice for two weeks, and the thought of her moving away was gut-wrenching. He almost wished there was still more to be done at the house. It would only take a few more days to sort through the rest of Louise's things. Alice had already scheduled a cleaning crew for the following week, and then the floors would be refinished. Once that was done, a photographer would come to take pictures of the house for the real estate listing...

Two weeks, max, and Alice would have completed what she came here to do.

Todd tore his gaze away from Alice and turned to his brother.

"Hey, I was wondering if you could build a play stand for a large parrot."

"For your girlfriend?" Jeff's tone was casual, but Todd felt his cheeks heat.

"Nah, she's not a parrot. The stand would be for Barnaby, the great green macaw."

"Barnaby the Great, huh?" Jeff's gaze flashed to Alice and back to his brother.

"Ideally, it would have perches of different diameters. Maybe a ladder to climb, some places to hang toys?"

"Sounds like a fun project," Jeff said, warming to the idea. "Maybe I could find some natural branches in cool shapes, just take the bark off and sand it down."

"It would be great if you could incorporate a concrete perch to wear down his nails. I can buy one online, and maybe a swing?"

"Sure, I'm game."

"Thanks!"

"No problem. Hey, go there," he told Beth.

"You play!" She shoved the game in front of Jeff and swiped the last of his pumpkin pie.

"Hey!" Jeff laughed.

She stole his fork.

"Longest road!" Alice announced from the other end of the room.

"You win," Max acknowledged. "Rematch!"

"Sure! I love this game."

"I'm out," Stephanie said cheerfully. "You girls have fun."

"I'll try!" Beth volunteered, running to the other end of the table.

It was amazing how easily she fit in, Todd thought. The little cousin they'd never had. It was nice to see Aunt Anna gelling so easily with her new sister and niece after the shock she'd had. *The Sullivan clan was quick to accept new members when they were a good fit.*

He stood up with a sigh and went into the kitchen in search of another beer. His mother was at the kitchen counter, wrapping leftovers.

"You should be out there enjoying yourself," he told her.

"No one's leaving anytime soon," she said. "I can't go to bed with a mess in the kitchen, and I don't want to be in here tonight. Anyway, Ethan and Mick took care of the dishes. I just need to finish this and then clean the counters."

Todd grabbed a sponge and rinsed it to handle the job.

"I like Alice a lot," she blurted.

He looked up in surprise. "Yeah," he said with a nod. "Me too."

"I can tell." She gave him such a knowing look that he ducked his head and focused all his energy on scrubbing a bit of hardened cheese off of the countertop.

"I'm trying not to fall in love," he admitted quietly.

Stephanie laughed.

"What?" he demanded.

"Oh, my sweet boy, that ship has sailed. You'd be better off using that energy to figure out how to get her to stay."

Todd stared at her in surprise. Was he in *love* with Alice? How was that even possible?

"We haven't known each other that long..."

"I know."

"I never believed in love at first sight," he told his mother.

"I know," she said again.

"I thought it was a stupid trope. I *hated* Romeo and Juliet."

"Lucky for you this isn't a Romeo-and-Juliet situation. I promise not to start a blood feud with Louise Fredrickson."

"I've never been in love," Todd said, feeling a little dizzy at the thought.

"Not even with Chelsea?"

"Not really," he admitted with a shrug. "I cared about her, and she cared about me, but when things ended, neither of us were brokenhearted."

"I didn't think so. Sit with me for a minute, would you?" His mother picked up her glass of wine and led him to the breakfast nook.

When they sat, she leaned in and searched his face, as if looking for answers. "Why haven't you asked her to stay?"

"I don't have anything to offer her," Todd said softly.

"You're an amazing catch. You're handsome, funny, smart, hardworking...How can you say that?"

"You hit it on the head with the last one. I work seventy hours a week, Mom. And then I go home, read case studies, plan for improvements on the clinic, and try to do some laundry before I go to bed and get up to do it all over again the next week. I'm not complaining. I love my work. But I don't have time for a girlfriend. I can't ask her to move here just for me. Especially given how long we've known each other."

"When you know, you know," she said quietly, looking out the window at the fat, autumn moon. "Your dad and I were so happy, but we didn't see each other much for a lot of those years. We worked so hard to build our careers, and then we had you guys. We told ourselves that when we retired, we'd be able to enjoy time together...really reap the fruits of our labor. We had such plans, Todd." She looked at him, and he saw tears in her eyes. "We were going to see Europe. Your dad wanted to do a whole second honeymoon to celebrate retirement. We were going to walk the Camino de Santiago in Spain, ride a gondola in Venice... Then, when we got back, we were going to build a greenhouse and plant a garden. He wanted to learn guitar," she laughed, brushing tears from her eyes.

"Only, you never got those days," Todd finished for her. His eyes stung, and his throat felt tight and achy.

"We never did." A tear slid down her cheek, and she took his hand. "That girl is out there today. Right now. Don't fool yourself into thinking you're promised a lifetime of tomorrows. There are no promises, Todd. Not for any of us."

"I know, Mom." He squeezed her hand.

"Do you?" Stephanie wiped her face. "You're a grown man now, so you do what you think is right. I just want you to know that I have everything I need. I'm not rich, but I'm financially secure enough that if the clinic went belly up, I could downsize the house and live a very comfortable life. I don't need anything from you, not financially. I just need to know that my kids are living full, well-rounded lives. Find

CHRISTINE GAEL

some balance, Todd. Because girls like that...that will make you feel the way she clearly makes you feel inside? Don't come along often." She stood up and kissed him on the forehead. "I'll stop preaching, now. Just think about what I've said over the next few days and consider it. Happy Thanksgiving, son."

"Happy Thanksgiving, Mom," Todd murmured, brain reeling as she walked away.

His mother was right. He would be a fool to let Alice go without telling her how he felt.

And his mother didn't raise a fool.

20

CEE-CEE

Cee-cee slotted the last of the dishes into her dishwasher and closed it. Mick had made an awesome brunch while she was down in the basement preparing that day's cupcakes. She had come upstairs to find the kitchen table loaded with broiled grapefruit, hash browns, sautéed veggies, and scrambled eggs. He was frying French toast as she walked in the door. As she sat down, Mick had poured them each a mimosa.

"What's the occasion?" she asked.

"The final Saturday of the month?" Mick shrugged and smiled. "Another day together is occasion enough."

They had enjoyed a leisurely meal just the two of them. And once the dishes were loaded, she had nothing to do all day but laze around with her fiancé.

What a luxury.

She started the dishwasher with the press of a button and went to join Mick on the couch. Tilly jumped up next to her. Cee-cee stroked her dog's velvety ears and leaned into Mick, looking out her big picture window at the

November waves lapping at the shore. The sky was pale blue, not a cloud to be seen, and the sea sparkled like a sapphire.

It was a perfect day, save for her niggling worries about Nate's financial troubles. God forbid that Max's holiday be spoiled by her father landing himself in the hospital, or the birth of Gabe and Sasha's daughter be overshadowed by a vicious attack on her grandfather. She needed to break the news to Max so she knew what was going on... and so she wouldn't worry that her father was ill or suicidal. Cee-cee wanted to let her daughter enjoy this break from work, but was it any better to tell her when she was busy with the bookshop? Or nearing Christmas?

"I can hear the wheels grinding in your head," Mick told her.

"Sorry." Cee-cee buried her face in his chest.

"You have to let go sometimes. You can't fix everything for everyone. Though, I do love that you always try," he added, kissing the top of her head.

"I know," she sighed. "I just can't help worrying about my kids. It's biological."

He squeezed her arm and they were silent for a moment, looking out at the waves. Cee-cee's phone rang from the bedroom, an obnoxious commercial jingle that Max had set it to as a joke. Cee-cee still hadn't figured out how to change it. She was tempted to ignore it... but what if it was one of her sisters, or the kids?

She extricated herself from between Mick and Tilly and stood up with a groan. These early mornings weren't getting any easier... It was time to hire a baker to come in a few days a week. Maybe after the holidays... Anna's name flashed over the screen, and Cee-cee answered just before it went to voicemail.

"Hi, Anna, what's up?"

"Beckett and I are headed to the movies tonight. The theater is screening an old James Dean film, one night only. Are you in?"

"That sounds like fun, but no. I need a night in. Mick and I are just going to watch a couple episodes of the TV series we have going and then go to bed early."

"Okay, old lady."

"This old lady is up at four every day to bake cupcakes."

"I know, I know. Well, they're screening something every Saturday for the rest of the year. Next week is The Sound of Music."

"That was Max's favorite movie when she was little," Cee-cee remembered, sitting down on her bed. Her fingers traced the lines of the quilt that she had made out of Max and Gabe's childhood clothes.

"I know, I was there. Occasionally. I brought her that Von Trapp dress from Austria."

"She wore it three Halloweens in a row," Cee-cee laughed, finding a patch made from that familiar fabric. "We should all go see it."

"Are you sure?" Anna said. "It starts at seven. You think you can stay awake?"

"Ha-ha," Cee-cee said flatly. She heard a knock to the door — which was strange, since not many people came upstairs to her apartment — but Mick would get it. "Hey, it was really nice seeing Nikki and Beth over the holiday. Beth fit right in."

"She did, didn't she? I'm a big fan, myself."

"Jeff loved having someone there close to his own age. I think he feels like the odd man out sometimes."

"It's no picnic being the youngest," said Anna.

"Yeah, and being the first-born is such a walk in the park," Cee-cee laughed.

Mick appeared in the doorway and held up a finger. "Sorry to bug you when you're chatting, but you have a visitor."

She lifted the phone away from her mouth. "Really? Who is it?"

"Nate. He said he preferred to wait outside..."

"Nate is *here*?"

"*Nate* is there?" Anna exclaimed. "Why?"

The same question was burning a hole in her mind as she straightened.

"Let me call you back later," Cee-cee told her.

"I want details!" Anna demanded a second before Cee-cee hung up.

"Why would he come here?" she wondered out loud.

"Only one way to find out," Mick said gruffly. "I asked him if whatever crap he's involved in could get you hurt, and he swore to me that it wouldn't. So go talk to him. I'm good."

Cee-cee smiled at him as she stood. She loved that he was protective, but also supportive and trusting. What a man.

She slipped on a pair of shoes and touched a hand to Mick's cheek as she walked past.

"I love you and I like you," she told him. It was a line from the silly sitcom they were watching here and there when they needed to unwind.

"I love you and I like you, too," Mick said. "Go on."

Nate was waiting for her in the hallway bundled in a navy pea-coat, looking sharp as ever. He seemed to have lost that hunted look, and the worry lines and tired eyes were gone.

"Thank you, Celia," he said before she could even greet him.

Cee-cee frowned at him and cocked her head. "For what?"

"I know you set things up with Ian, and I just wanted to come and thank you face to face. After what I put you through, you certainly didn't have to do that, but I appreciate it more than you know. You saved my bacon. I won't ever forget it."

She stared at him and crossed her arms over her chest. "Nate, I have no idea what you're talking about."

It was Nate's turn to frown in confusion. "The loan."

"Ian is giving you a loan?" she demanded, her tone high-pitched and reedy with surprise.

Nate pulled back and nodded cautiously. "Yeah. He called me yesterday and offered to loan me the money I need, using the equity in the house as collateral. I have a year to pay him back, which is plenty of time to get the new condos profitable and get back on my feet. When I asked him why he was doing that, he said he was doing it for Max and for you. I asked if Max knew and he said no, so I just assumed that you asked him..." Nate trailed off.

"No." Cee-cee was stunned. "I didn't ask him. I would *never* have asked him to loan you that kind of money."

God, she wouldn't ask *anyone* in the family to loan this man a dime. It brought tears to her eyes to know that Max had found someone who cared for her so deeply.

Nate looked as puzzled as she'd felt when he'd first opened his mouth. "If you didn't ask him, then why?"

She thought back to their her very brief conversation with Ian on Thanksgiving. "He is just an amazing, intuitive guy who's crazy about our daughter and didn't want her...or me, to worry, I guess. How lucky are we?"

Nate's shoulders slumped.

"Lucky. But it's humbling," he said quietly, "taking a loan from Max's boyfriend. But I don't have much of a choice. I'll never do anything like that again, Celia, I swear. I don't want to give you any more grief than I already have, and I definitely don't want to be a burden on the kids."

"I know."

"I'm going to spend the rest of my life making it up to them... and looking for another woman like you. If I ever find one, I'm going to be a man who deserves her. I'm sorry, Celia. For everything. I hope you're happy with Mick. I really do."

"Thank you, Nate."

He turned to go, and a sudden thought occurred to Cee-cee.

"Hey, Nate?"

"Yeah?"

"Do you remember Maryanne Carpenter Brown?"

Nate thought for a moment. "Blonde? Had some kind of beef with Anna?"

"That's the one."

"Why?"

"She's changed a lot, too. Sasha did some work for her on her new house, and she was really sweet to her. Maryanne's looking for someone special, and trying to be worthy of them this time around... Maybe reach out. It never hurts to make a friend."

Nate stared at her. "Are you seriously trying to set me up right now? Is that what it's come to? My ex is pimping me out now?"

"I wouldn't go that far," Cee-cee chuckled. "Just a thought."

"Thank you. For everything." He held her eyes for one long moment, the air between them thick with memories of the three decades that they had spent together. Then, he turned and walked down the stairs.

Cee-cee walked back into her apartment, where Mick sat whittling something. He rarely whittled inside, but the carving knife came out sometimes when he was nervous. He set down the knife and the wooden block and looked up at Cee-cee.

"How did it go?"

"Great, actually," she said, still in shock. "Come back to the couch, would you?"

They walked around to the couch and she snuggled up to him as she filled him in.

"So now Nate has a whole year to get back on his feet," she finished with a relived sigh. "Remind me to send a couple dozen cupcakes to Ian's escape room later. He saved the day."

Mick held her closer. "And do you feel settled?"

"I do," Cee-cee told him, resting her head on his chest.

"That's the important thing."

"All's well with the Sullivan clan," she said with satisfaction.

"Do you feel settled enough to finally set a date?"

"For our wedding?" Cee-cee sat up.

"I'm getting impatient," said Mick with a self-deprecating chuckle.

"You and me both," she said whole-heartedly. "So let's not delay. How about in the spring? As soon as the snow is gone, Grace has been born, and Sasha has a little time to recover."

"Just name the time and place."

Cee-cee leaned back into him with a sigh.

"None of that matters to me as long as it's with you."

It was only November, and already this was turning out to be an amazing holiday season.

2 1

TODD

T ODD LEANED AGAINST HIS J EEP, watching painters spruce up Aunt Louise's house with a bright new coat of whitewash. The realtor had been by that morning to do an appraisal and make recommendations regarding what needed fixing before she would show the place. Alice had texted Todd in some distress, saying that the realtor had insisted that Barnaby and his cage be moved out before the first showing.

Todd jogged up the front steps, his mind full of things that he wanted to say. All morning at the clinic, snatches of imagined conversation had filled his head.

I realize we've only known each other a short time, but please keep me in mind as you make this major life decision.

He groaned internally as he knocked on the door.

Alice greeted him with a smile, but her eyes were bloodshot.

"What's wrong?" he asked gently.

"Nothing." She plopped down on the newly cleaned velvet sofa and blew out a sigh. "Everything."

The house was tidy, and she was dressed in red corduroy pants and a fitted yellow t-shirt. His heart beat faster.

"Was it your meeting with the realtor?" He sat next to her. "Is the house not in good enough shape?"

"It's not that." Alice groaned. "The house is actually worth a lot of money. I just hate to let it go. Auntie *loves* this house, and she loves Barnaby even more."

At the sound of his name, the great green macaw came flying in from the kitchen. He landed on the back of the couch near Alice and gently took one of her curls in his beak.

"Holy cow!" Todd exclaimed in awe. "He looks great."

"I've mostly been leaving the door to his cage open." Alice's tone was bittersweet. She reached up and ruffled the feathers on the back of Barnaby's neck. The bird closed his eyes in pleasure as Alice scratched his head.

"He likes you," Todd said in wonder. "Feels like we were just trying to figure out how to open the cage without him taking our eyes out."

"He was scared," Alice said softly, still petting the bird. "He's a good boy."

She dropped her hand and looked at Todd with an expression of growing despair.

"How can I tell her she has to give him up? There has to be a way to reunite him with Aunt Louise."

"You want to call Auntie?" Barnaby asked in a voice eerily similar to Alice's.

"I know you miss her." Alice reached to pet Barnaby's head again.

"There's a parrot sanctuary in Harmony," Todd told her.

"Is that in Maine?"

"Yeah, it's not too far from here. You could bring Louise

to visit him, when she's well enough for a day trip. He's probably going to outlive her, Alice. I don't know exactly how old he is, but some macaws can live for over seventy years. Siesta Sanctuary offers a permanent home for parrots whose owners can't care for them anymore."

Alice was shaking her head.

"That's great, Todd. Truly. But they've been together for so long...I still think it will break both of their hearts. I've been racking my brain and I just don't know what to do."

She wasn't wrong. Parrots often bonded with their owners, and without them, sometimes had trouble bonding with other birds. There was even a name for the phenomenon. The "one-person bird." Even now, as much as Barnaby seemed to like Alice well enough, Todd had the distinct sense Louise was his "one person."

"It's just really sad, that's all."

She sounded close to tears and Todd wanted nothing more than to gather her up in his arms and hold her.

"The stocks you found won't cover in-home care for awhile?"

"They're worth a lot," Alice replied listlessly, folding her hands in her lap. "Over twenty thousand, but that would just buy some time. My uncle does okay, but he doesn't have the kind of cash to pay for a ramp to make the steps easier, and day to day help." She met Todd's eyes, and he could hear his pulse pounding in his ears. "No matter what, I really appreciate all of your help," Alice said earnestly. She gave him a kiss on the cheek and didn't move away. A second later, his lips were on hers.

The scent of lemons surrounded him as he got lost in

Alice. One of his hands still held hers. The other brushed her cheek, moved into hair –

"Ouch!" Todd jerked back in surprise.

"What is it?" Alice asked him, brows high on her forehead.

Todd examined his hand; a drop of blood welled up below the first finger.

"Barnaby bit me."

"You are the weakest link," said the parrot in a severe British accent. "Goodbye."

Alice giggled, one hand over her mouth.

"I gave you fruit...and toys," Todd told the bird, and Alice laughed outright. She leaned forward and kissed him again, a quick peck on the lips, and then she sat back with a sigh. Barnaby went back to grooming her curls, keeping a watchful eye on Todd.

When the words finally came, they came out in a rush.

"Don't go," he blurted. He cleared his throat and tried again, in a more measured tone, "I don't want you go."

"I don't *want* to go. My lease is up in a week." Alice's tone was regretful, and she smiled sadly and reached out to take his hand. "The house will sell fast, and I don't have anywhere to live."

"There are so many empty vacation rentals in the wintertime. I'm sure we could find something affordable and I know I can find you work, either with my Aunt Cee-cee or maybe at Ian's escape room. You'd have a place of your own, no shouting roommates. And I'm going to cut back at work," he added in a rush. "My mom keeps telling me to find some balance, and she's right. I'm going to hire someone, either a part-time veterinarian or a full time vet tech. I know it's asking a lot, but... Alice, I hardly slept last night, thinking of letting you walk away."

"I want to stay, but—" Alice began, and her phone began to buzz. She took back her hand. "Sorry, just a minute. Hello, this is Alice," she answered.

Her eyebrows rose as a male voice chattered excitedly in the background.

"Okay. And how much is that?" she paused for a long moment and let out a gasp.

"Thousand?"

Her shocked eyes locked on Todd and his adrenaline started pumping. It took everything he had not to press his head next to hers so he could eavesdrop.

"All right. Um, that sounds great. I look forward to hearing from you soon!"

She disconnected and shook her head slowly like she was in a daze. "Th-that was Mr. Phipps, the jeweler. I dropped Auntie Louise's stuff off yesterday for him to do an appraisal. He finally finished going through it all and said that even the costume stuff was vintage...but the ruby ring we found?"

Todd nodded and leaned forward. "Yeah?"

"It's from the late eighteen hundreds, apparently. One of a kind. He has a call in to an auction house but he estimates it could be worth—" she broke off and swallowed audibly. "Over a hundred thousand dollars."

"Holy crap," Todd murmured. "That's amazing."

"I have to call Auntie," Alice said, lifting the phone in her trembling hand. "Auntie Louise?" Alice said when the call connected. "I heard back from the jeweler." She explained what he'd told her, and the silence as deafening. A second later, a *whoop* loud enough to for Todd to hear echoed through the room.

Alice laughed and held the phone away from her ear.

"So you want to sell it?" Alice confirmed.

"Of course I want to sell it!" Louise shouted exuberantly. Todd lost track of the conversation as the old lady's voice dropped to a normal register, but Alice's wide grin was enough for him.

"Okay, Auntie," she said at last. "That sounds real good to me. I'll keep you posted. I love you too."

She disconnected and then set her phone onto the coffee table, and caught Todd in a crushing hug. Her slender arms were surprisingly strong, and the smell of her hair temporarily robbed him of the power of speech.

"What a godsend," she said as she released him. Tears sparkled in her eyes.

"A Christmas miracle come early," Todd agreed.

"Between all of the jewelry and the stocks, she'd be able to come home to Barnaby if she had someone to keep the place up and help with meals." Alice smiled shyly. "She, um, she asked me if I'd be willing to be that person. I'm thinking a starving artist should be willing to work for room and board until she can find a place of her own..."

"You mean it?" Todd demanded.

"It would be easy to stay in Bluebird Bay if I didn't have to pay rent until I had a good job. I wouldn't even have to write those boring blog posts anymore. I could be here for Auntie during the day and play music at night... maybe write one of the novels that have been kicking around in my head. Then, when I move out, I just have to make sure I'm close enough to stop by every day and help out. I don't mind."

Unable to hold back his excitement another second, Todd stood and pulled Alice to her feet, a safe distance from the parrot. He kissed her, lifting her feet off the floor for a moment before setting her down again.

"I can't wait to hear you play," he said, and kissed her forehead. "And read your book." He kissed her cheek. "And take you sledding." He kissed the corner of her mouth. "And show you Bluebird Bay in the summertime. I...I think I love you, Alice Nielson. I know it sounds crazy, but--"

She stood on tiptoe and kissed him full on the lips.

"It doesn't sound crazy to me. Because I think I love you, too, Dr. Ketterman."

Blood rushed in his ears as he stared down at her. How had he gotten so lucky?

"The tribe has spoken!" Barnaby intoned.

Alice broke away, laughing. Her eyes were bright as she looked up at Todd.

"I suppose it has."

NIKKI

"I'm glad you came," Nikki told her daughter as she took the exit for Portland International Airport, "and I'm glad we stayed in Bluebird Bay for Thanksgiving."

"Me too," Beth said. "That was so much fun, especially all the board games they had. And Jeff is really cool — we're going to play online games together when I get back to my dorm."

"They're good people."

"They are." Beth let out an explosive sigh. "What a weird month. I lost the dad that I never really had to begin with, but I gained this whole other family. I know Aunt Anna's our only blood relative, but... well, if felt just like a family holiday at Aunt Lena's place. I'm sad I didn't get to see Grandpa this trip, but it was nice to skip Uncle Jack's annual Thanksgiving lecture. 'The girl needs a father figure,'" Beth mimicked. "'I didn't sign up for the job, but someone has to keep her in line.'"

Nikki grimaced and chuckled at the same time. Her eyes

were on the road, but she could picture Jack's scowl on Beth's cherubic face.

"He means well," she told her daughter.

"Satan probably meant well, too."

"Beth!" Nikki exclaimed. "You did not just compare your Uncle Jack to the devil himself."

"I'm just saying," Beth grumbled, "Everyone thinks their actions are justified."

"Your uncle loves you. He loves us both. He just needs-"

"A medical procedure to pull the stick out of his butt," Beth cut in, her tone matter of fact.

"Stop it!" Nikki gasped as she pulled into the cell-phone lot. "That's enough about your Uncle Jack for today."

She put the car in park and let it idle, not ready for the rushed goodbye at the departure's curb. As well as she'd been doing since Beth had left for school, it was hard to have her back for a short time and watch her go again.

She turned to look her daughter in the eye.

"I'm sorry I didn't tell you sooner," she said. "About everything."

"That was really lame." Beth's face closed off for a moment as she retreated inward. "But I forgive you."

"It was. It was really lame. And I won't do it again."

"We're not going to be living together for a long time... maybe ever," Beth told her, and suddenly Nikki's eyes were hot with tears. "Not seeing me in person isn't an excuse not to tell me things, okay? If you want to tell me something face to face, just do a video call."

Nikki wiped the tears from her eyes as she nodded. "Deal."

Beth's eyes went glassy and she let out a snort. "Oh my God! Stop crying. You're making my eyes fill up with empathy tears," she blustered, bringing a smile to Nikki's face. "This is barely goodbye, Mom. I'll see you in less than a month for Christmas."

"In Cherry Blossom Point," Nikki promised.

"Good. I miss Grandpa a lot, and I'm knitting Christmas presents for everyone. Even Uncle Jack. Just a plain navy-blue hat, but that's all he'd wear anyway. Grandpa and Aunt Gayle get patterned hats, and I'm knitting a rainbow scarf for Aunt Lena."

"Anything for me?"

"It's a surprise! You get the nicest wool, this baby-soft merino dyed really gorgeous colors. That yarn shop by my school is eating up so much of my money that I might have to get a job there. I was so bummed that I forgot all of my knitting stuff when I packed for Bluebird Bay, but I was in such a daze... usually when I binge watch a TV show I'm at least doing something productive at the same time."

"I can't believe you spent all of your money on Christmas gifts months in advance," Nikki said, her eyes misting over again, this time with pride. "And handmaking them...really thoughtful."

"The gifts are just an excuse to do fun projects," Beth told her self-consciously. "Knitting is like a meditation for me, and trying new patterns is really fun."

Nikki leaned forward to gather her daughter in her arms. For such a tough, independent girl who wasn't going to miss her mother at all, she hugged Nikki back awfully hard before pulling away.

"Okay, enough," the girl laughed. "Call as much as you'd

like. Would you please drive me the rest of the way? I'm going to miss my flight."

"You have plenty of time," Nikki said, but she put the car in drive and slowly pulled out of the airport waiting area. She parked beneath the Departures sign and pulled Beth in for one last crushing squeeze.

"I love you so much," she told her daughter.

"I love you too, Mom. I'll see you soon."

And just like that, Beth was gone again. Nikki felt like she was missing a piece of her. It was such a bewildering mix of emotions, every time. Love, pride, grief, freedom. She was lighter, she was bereaved. She pulled away from the airport and headed for the highway.

She had devoted her entire adult life to Beth. Who would she be without her? She was starting to figure it out, but she still had a foot on each side of a chasm. There was her life in Cherry Blossom Point, her aging father, the house she had shared with Beth, the sisters that she'd grown up with... and then there was her new life in Bluebird Bay. Mateo, Anna and the Sullivan clan.

How would she integrate the two? She couldn't keep bouncing back and forth, living two lives. Not forever, anyway.

Beth's comment echoed in her head. *"We're not going to be living together for a long time...maybe ever."*

There was this summer, at least. Beth would come home from school. But next year, who knew? Kids stayed on campus for summer school or jobs, they studied abroad or moved away for internships... even summers weren't a guarantee. So what was she staying in Cherry Blossom Point for?

There was her father. The thought of moving in his golden years, even a couple hours away, tore at her heart. But lord, the man had four other children... that she knew of. Three that lived less than twenty minutes away from him. Gayle and Lena both doted on the man just as much as she did. And if Jack wanted to take control of the family so badly, let *him* take over Dad's care.

It wasn't like she was considering moving across the country. She could still visit him on her days off.

Her thoughts drifted to Mateo. He was great, and she couldn't wait to see how things developed between them. But she had been in an awful, codependent relationship with Steve from the time she'd left her parent's house until she'd left with Beth. Her father looked after them, her sisters worried over her, Jack hovered like a disapproving parole officer...

She'd never really felt in charge of her own destiny. Her life felt almost like it had been decided on by committee until she'd broken the chain of command and went to Bluebird Bay. There, she'd been able to do what she wanted to do without having to explain herself. She could stretch her wings and fly. Sure, sometimes she'd crashed and burned, but she'd also soared. As much as she loved Cherry Blossom Point, she wasn't sure if she could reinvent her relationships with her siblings enough to have that there.

Plus, the thought of saying goodbye to Anna just as they were really getting to know each other was hard. She wanted more long talks with her sister, more hikes and shared meals.

Nikki's phone dinged as she neared Bluebird Bay, and she checked her messages at a red light.

Are you back from the airport yet? Anna asked.

Nearly, Nikki answered.

Can you meet me at the diner in twenty?

She checked the car's clock radio. There was time to stop for lunch before meeting Mateo back at the Airbnb to clear out the last of her stuff.

Sure.

Twenty minutes later, she slid into a booth at Mo's and shot her sister a questioning glance.

"Just had a hankering for a turkey club or?"

"Actually, no," her sister replied. "Um...what time are you heading back to Cherry Blossom Point?"

Nikki shrugged. "I'm trying to get on the road no later than five." She reached for a menu and then paused to study Anna for a long moment. "Why?"

Anna's lips tipped into a grim smile. "Because I'm coming with you."

Come to Cherry Blossom Point and meet the Merrill's in Starting From Scratch, out June 20th, 2021!

Join Anna Sullivan as she leaves Bluebird Bay and travels to Cherry Blossom Point to meet the family she never knew she had...

When Nikki Merrill set off to find her long lost sister, she never imagined she'd be returning home to Cherry Blossom Point with her in tow. Battle lines are drawn when each of her siblings have wildly different reactions to their new family member. Lena is willing to invite Anna into their lives, Gayle can't even look at her, and all their brother Jack can see is another heir looking for a piece of the pie.

And Nikki?

She's caught dead in the middle of things.

If she continues to build her relationship with Anna, will it splinter the one she has with the siblings she's always known?

Anna Sullivan didn't want a new sister. Now that she has one, though, she's in for the long haul. When she heads to Cherry Blossom Point to spend some time with Nikki and meet the rest of the family, she isn't prepared for the drama that ensues. It's kind of hard to make a good impression when half her new siblings see her as a walking representation of their father's infidelity. And when more family secrets are uncovered, she realizes they've only seen the tip of the iceberg.

Will Anna figure out how to navigate these choppy family waters, or will her visit to Cherry Blossom Point turn out to be a disaster of Titanic proportions?

ALSO BY CHRISTINE GAEL

Want to get an alert next time a new Bluebird Bay book is out, find out about sales or contests, and chat with Christine? Join the mailing list **here!**

Maeve's Girls

(Standalone Women's Fiction)

Bluebird Bay

Finding Tomorrow

Finding Home

Finding Peace

Finding Forever

Finding Forgiveness

Finding Acceptance

Finding Redemption

Cherry Blossom Point

Starting From Scratch

Lucky Strickland Series (Mystery/Thriller)

Lucky Break

Getting Lucky

Crow's Feet Coven (Paranormal Women's Fiction)

Writing Wrongs

Brewing Trouble

Stealing Time

Made in the USA
Columbia, SC
01 July 2021

41253175R00138